Praise for K. I and Baby Steps

"*Baby Steps* is a heartwarming story about a woman's ability to overcome a severe loss and move on with her life. The characters are well developed and their interactions with each other range from thought provoking to humorously entertaining. This is an all around great book to read."

~*ReaderViews*

"A quick, light read, *Baby Steps* is the story of a woman starting her life over in the most sane and responsible way she can."

~*Monday Magazine*

" McLoughlin [demonstrates] remarkable restraint and compassion in her story... [She] throws in an ending with a shocking twist too. She certainly isn't pulling any punches with her first foray into book publishing. The characters are also well developed.... You have to admire McLoughlin's aplomb."

~*Parksville Qualicum Beach News*

"Life is never fair - and never let anyone tell you otherwise. *Baby Steps* is Lynda Blake's story of the troubles of being the single mother of a teenage son - an adventure in itself - and trying to take care of her own life. *Baby Steps* is highly recommended!"

~*Midwest Book Review*

"Mc Loughlin has packed a lot of juicy goodness into a fun, quick read!"

~ *Victoria - Romance Writer's of America*

"*Baby Steps* is the perfect beach book!"

~*Sasha Cooper*

"I did enjoy reading a novel by a spiritual, political woman unafraid to state her beliefs."

~*Catherine Duthie*

Baby Steps

To my Birthday Buddy Shaug! Have a blast in Spain! I'll be thinking of you reading my book while soaking up the sun! Hope you like it! Cheers, K~

K. L. Mc Loughlin

Baby Steps

K. L. McLoughlin

Langdon Street Press

Langdon Street Press
212 3rd Avenue North, Suite 570
Minneapolis, MN 55401
1.888.645.5248
www.langdonstreetpress.com

ISBN - 978-0-9799120-9-2
ISBN - 0-9799120-9-1
LCCN - 2008921827

LANGDON STREET PRESS

Book sales for North America and international:
Itasca Books, 3501 Highway 100 South, Suite220
Minneapolis, MN 55416
Phone: 952.345.4488 (toll free 1.800.901.3480)
Fax: 952.920.0541; email to orders@itascabooks.com

Cover Design and typeset by James/Dzyn Lab

Printed in the United States of America

Acknowledgments

To my husband Michael, you make all my dreams come true! Your love and support mean everything to me. I have never felt as beautiful as I do when you look at me.

To all the many friends and family who have suffered through the early drafts;

To Kwrites, I still owe you a round of golf;

To M.M., J.W., A.S., and all the people at Mill City;

To A., without your copyedit I never would have shown the manuscript to anyone in the industry;

And To Tasha, You made me see myself as an artist. Your painstaking, loving criticism was an incredible and precious gift;

Thank you all!

Chapter 1

Lynda was fussing with the hors d'oeuvres for the tenth time, checking the flowers and decorations with more than her usual pre-entertaining nerves. But then this was no ordinary party. Months ago she had promised herself that somehow she would find a way back to the living but surely there had to be a better way than this! At least Sean, her seventeen-year-old son, was safely away at his friend Paul's house for the next several hours. She still wasn't sure how she had been talked into hosting this event. It was the third glass of wine that had done her in. Clearly three glasses of wine was past her limit because it was after that, that she had made the smart ass comment to the girls, "What exactly is an adult toy anyway?" Now here she was, despite being celibate since her husband's death over two years ago, hosting a pleasure party of all things. The girls had better damn well show up and not leave her alone with all that 'stuff', she thought. At the very least it would make good material for one of her bodice ripper novels. She'd never imagined beginning a new career as a romance novelist in her forties but this was probably the only good thing that came from David's death, the financial freedom to pursue her dream of writing. The pain of losing David was only bearable because miraculously Sean had escaped from the car accident unscathed. Channeling all that pain, all the lost dreams into her writing and knowing her son would live a long healthy life kept her going.

Lingerie, lotions and toys—some of which she wasn't sure she wanted to understand—filled her living room. Madonna's VH-2 collection was thumping in the background and she was surrounded by honey dust and handcuffs and that pink bumpy vibrating ring thing. She wondered yet again, how did this happen to me.

"David, this is all your fault," she muttered to herself.

Heather, the minister's wife, almost spit out her wine as she laughed. "Really, Lynda, David's been gone two years. I don't think you can blame hosting a pleasure party at your house on poor David, God rest his soul."

"Well, it certainly can't be my fault, can it? Besides, what exactly is clitoral stimulant anyway?" The little white bottle in her hand was promising almost-forgotten pleasures.

Rachel, the British expatriate educator for the evening, explained. It was amazing to Lynda how nothing sounded dirty in an English accent. Heather grabbed the test bottle out of Lynda's hands and headed to the bathroom.

"Let's see if this stuff really works," she said.

The ladies all laughed in wonder. "I think we should've advertised this as a way to get new parishioners," Charlotte said.

"The Episcopal Church wants you!" said Diane.

"Wants you!" cackled Shelly, Lynda's best friend.

"Wants you to be really happy!" Lynda added. "More wine, anyone?"

As several glasses rose into the air, Heather returned. "Oooh, it's like Icy Hot!"

"All right, girls," Rachel said as she returned to business. She had her products to sell after all. "Now, vibrators have come a long way in recent years."

Several of Lynda's friends nodded knowingly. Lynda said, "I feel like a virgin. I might as well be one. It's been two years since David died and only now am I buying my first vibrator."

"This one was quite popular; see how many directions it moves in," Rachel continued. "This is a good model for ummm …"

"Marital replacement therapy," said soon-to-be-divorced Shelly.

"Um, quite. Here, Lynda, hold this for a moment, will you, while I get some other models." Rachel searched in one of her big black bags of pleasure while she continued talking. "It is quite pretty. It's pink. It's got a bunny with ears that wiggle, the top few inches rotate around 360° and vibrate, and there are those beads for extra width."

Lynda smiled. "This has possibilities. Hey, I wonder what this button does? Oh my gosh, the whole thing is a vibrating orgasm machine."

Hoots of laughter filled Lynda's house as her jaw dropped and her eyes widened. "What do you think, girls, should I get me one of these?"

Click.

"That was the front door closing, right?" she said.

Everyone quickly looked down at their toes; their shoulders shaking with barely contained laughter as Lynda turned around to face her 6'2" 17-year-old son. He towered over her little 5'4" body, looking at the big pink bunny vibrator humming in her hand.

He closed his blue-gray eyes tightly and said, "I don't want to know."

Lynda's face felt hot to the touch. "Okay, we'll talk later."

"Hope not," he said, as he politely raced to his room.

Lynda sank into the nearest seat, vibrator still humming. "I think I'll have another glass of wine now."

A few hours later, as Lynda finished cleaning up the last of the dishes from her inaugural Pleasure Party, she looked around her home—the home that she and David had loved so much. This was the home that they bought art for together, the home that they brought Sean home from the hospital to, the home that they lived, loved, fought, and made up in. It was her home now—hers and Sean's, but really it was hers. The only thing she'd changed was the new bedroom set she'd bought herself a couple of months ago. She'd always wanted a big four-poster bed and she loved having girly sheets and shams and comforters on it. She loved filling her bedroom with the fresh scent of lavender.

"Oh, quit stalling," she said to herself as she wrung the dishtowel in her hands for the tenth time. She squared her shoulders and with a final sigh, mounted a half flight of stairs in her split-level home to Sean's room.

She knocked on his door.

"Is dinner ready yet? I'm starved," Sean said as he opened the door, not quite meeting his mother's eye.

"No. You were supposed to be at Paul 's for dinner, remember? But you can scavenge in the kitchen later."

"Something came up with his girlfriend and he bailed on me," Sean said.

Lynda paused. "We should talk."

Sean shifted his weight from side to side, his eyes darting around, searching for escape. Finding none, he began to retreat. "Really," he blurted, "Mom, it's okay. I mean, I tried not to think about it—hard not to, but I mean I guess it's okay for you to … Well, I don't know what exactly, but that's good too. I mean I'll respect your privacy …" He backed into his bed and slumped down on it.

Lynda walked into his room and pulled his desk chair out and sat on it, facing her son.

"I'm glad you'll respect my privacy, but at the same time I want you to be okay with the fact that I need it." She took a deep breath and forced herself to look into her son's eyes, David's eyes. "You know I will always love your dad …"

"Mom, really, you don't have to do this, it's cool." His eyes begged her to stop.

"But he's dead. And, well, I'm not. And I have to find a way to live a full life. You're almost grown, almost gone, and I don't want to be alone forever. I liked being married. I liked being a woman."

"Oh God." Sean looked around in desperation.

Lynda sighed. "I don't want to be numb inside, and an important part of me almost died with your father. I'm trying to figure out how to bring it back to life. I may even want to start dating soon."

"Dating? Dating I can handle, I think." He paused. "Yeah, I can handle that. I mean, Dad would want you to be happy, but you better make sure you are treated well or I'll have something to say about it."

"I should hope so." She paused. "No one could ever replace your dad, you know."

"I know."

Lynda got up and turned to leave.

"Mom?"

"Yeah?"

"Was Reverend John's wife really here?"

"Yup!"

Sean got up to go to the kitchen.

"Do girls really … um … do … that?"

"Do what exactly?" Lynda smiled.

"Um, you know … take care of things themselves?"

"Some do, more should. Heaven knows it takes most men long enough to learn how a woman works, if they ever do." Lynda laughed to herself seeing Sean's stunned silence. She smiled as she went to the kitchen to feed her ever-hungry son. Things would really be okay after all.

Chapter 2

A s Lynda was filling her trunk with soda, near-beer and wine from Beverages & More, she couldn't help but notice the commotion of picketers across the street and some lunatic on a Megaphone forcing his views on the world around him. Pro-lifers were picketing in front of the Women's Clinic beside the Albertson's.

"Good Lord," she thought, "What are those people doing out here? Isn't Northern California supposed to be full of reasonable people or at least liberals?" Returning her gaze to the task at hand she paused as she saw a young woman alone in her car in the Albertson's parking lot, eyeing the picketers as she bit her nails. "Poor thing," Lynda muttered under her breath. A police car circled the clinic and parked. An officer and a detective got out of the car. The two men walked through the protestors and entered the clinic. A few moments later they returned to their car and drove off.

Being the good mom, good citizen, that she was; Lynda returned the BevMo cart to its proper place by the front door of the store. Keys in hand, she glanced once more at the blue Honda Civic in the Albertson's parking lot. The young woman was still there, still chewing on her fingertips.

Lynda bit her lower lip, not sure what she should do. Raising her eyes to heaven, she said, "Well, you're the one who made me so darn nosy and helpful." With that, she tossed her keys in her purse and headed across the four-lane road trying to find the right words to say.

Approaching the Civic from the driver's side, she saw that the young woman was young indeed, probably no older than Sean. The girl was staring intently at the picketers and jumped at the tap on her window.

"Mrs. B.?" she said.

"Hey, I know you, too. I'm sorry, I don't remember your name."

"I'm Maddie. I'm Paul's girlfriend."

"Of course. Sorry about that." She was Sean's best friend's girlfriend.

"Um, can I help you with something, Mrs. B.?"

"Actually, Maddie, I came over because I thought maybe you could use my help. Maybe going in there?" Lynda gestured towards the Women's Clinic.

Maddie flushed and looked down.

"Where's Paul?"

"He's late. Really late. I don't think he's coming."

"What do you want to do, Maddie?"

She sighed. Her shoulders sagged with her burden. "I need to go inside."

"You're sure?"

Maddie nodded, eyes glued to the floor.

"Then let's go," said Lynda.

Maddie looked up.

Lynda opened her car door. "C'mon, let's go."

Maddie got out of the car and locked it up. As Lynda and Maddie approached the clinic, the pro-lifers smelled fresh blood. Lynda put her right arm around Maddie and held her tight; with her left, she pushed her way through the crowd, through the insults that threatened damnation. The ringleader was tall and thin and male. He was smug and righteous in his conviction. His hair was straight, neat and his clothes were crisp and conservative. He was camera ready. Lynda recognized him on sight from his many sound bites on the news.

His voice grated as he turned to Maddie and said, "If you enter that house of sin you'll have to live with more than regret. You'll have to live knowing that you chose to commit murder, a mortal sin!" Naturally, he was unwilling to offer any real help or solutions. Instead his concern for Maddie's soul clearly ended at the clinic door. As they neared the front door, someone from inside opened it and ushered them in.

"Sorry about that," the woman said brusquely, "Ron Thompson is at it again."

She was tall and chic in a designer suit and had shiny, severe black hair. "Let me get you checked in. Please follow me." She led them through the small waiting room to the receptionist's window. "Do you have an appointment?"

"Yes," Maddie whispered, looking at the floor.

The woman just looked at Maddie, impatient. Glancing from one to the other, Lynda nudged Maddie.

"Maddie, she needs to have your name and who your appointment's with."

"Oh, sorry. I'm Madeleine Lacy and I have a two o'clock appointment with Dr. Cameron."

"Very well," the woman said, "Have a seat."

They sat together in the waiting room. "She seemed nice," Maddie said.

"Really? How do you figure?"

"She got the door for us. She's very businesslike and efficient. Maybe I'll be like that someday."

Lynda looked at Maddie strangely. "True, she got the door for us and I have nothing against businesslike and efficient, but don't you think she was a little cold?"

Maddie grinned ever so slightly. "Maybe if I was a little colder I wouldn't be in this mess."

Lynda chuckled despite herself. "I gotta love a girl with gallows humor."

Maddie turned and looked at Lynda. "Thanks, Mrs. B."

Lynda put her arm around the girl and hugged her. "You're welcome."

They listened as the roar of the crowd outside grew in anger. When the door opened, a woman in her mid thirties entered.

"Sorry I'm late, Susan. Ron Thompson is at it again out there," she said to the woman who had let Lynda and Maddie in.

Susan looked unforgivingly at the woman in jeans and a silk blouse, whose long curly hair refused to be tamed. "Carol, when you have a moment perhaps you could show Miss Lacy back to Dr. Cameron's office. She made it past Mr. Thompson and his megaphone and fellow picketers on time." Susan's tone was condescending to say the least.

"Of course, Ms. Costas," Carol said, unfazed. She turned to Maddie. "I'll just be a moment, Maddie. Sorry I'm late."

Maddie just smiled and nodded. A moment later Carol returned, beckoning Maddie to follow. Maddie got up and looked at Mrs. B., then back at Carol.

Lynda stood up. "May I come with Maddie?"

"Of course," Carol said. "I'm glad she has someone with her today. I'm sorry Paul couldn't be here too, Maddie."

"Me too," she said.

Carol led them into an office decorated with warm, cherry-wood bookcases and desk, a plush beige carpet, and comfortable stuffed chairs. She turned to Maddie and said, "Michael, sorry Dr. Michael Cameron will be here in a few moments. Today he'll want to talk to you again for as long as you need. He'll give you and your friend some information and counseling resources. I know this seems repetitive, but it's important information, and, of course, you have our number here if you need us, or any of this information again. After you've conferred with Dr. Michael you will be able to fill your Plan B prescription here if you decide to go forward but you will need to fill the prescriptions for pain killers at your normal pharmacy."

Without looking up, Maddie said, "Thanks, Carol."

Lynda squeezed Maddie's shoulder and turned to Carol. "Thank you, Carol. It's nice to know what to expect."

She nodded and closed the door behind her as she left. Maddie slumped in one of the chairs and Lynda sat in the one beside her. Maddie was silent and chewing on her bottom lip. Lynda watched her closely, not sure what to say.

Barely audibly she asked, "Mrs. B, do you think they're right?"

"Who?"

"The protesters outside. Do you think God will ever forgive me?" She had tears in her eyes.

"Oh, Maddie!" Lynda reached for Maddie's hands and took them in her own. Neither woman had heard the door open behind them. "God is a parent, Maddie. He feels your pain as intensely as you do." Maddie's tears started to roll down her cheeks. "If you ask me, God is more worried about whether or not you'll forgive yourself and move forward in your life."

Maddie raised her eyes and looked straight at Lynda. "You really think so?"

"Yes, I do. God loves you, Maddie. I may be a heretic but I doubt it. I mean, God is pretty definite about free will and, like any parent allowing a child to make big decisions, he or she may not always agree with what you do, but she's on your side and hopes you learn from your choices and grow. Think about it, Maddie. Who did Jesus hang with when he was here?"

Maddie actually chuckled. "Hang with—I've never thought about Jesus hanging!"

Lynda smiled. "C'mon, that's what He did. He walked around hanging out with people who wanted to listen to him. And he hung out mostly not with the powerful rabbis or the righteous. He hung out with the poor and troubled and the suffering. All kinds of people with screwed-up lives. And what did he offer them? He offered them love, Maddie, love."

The door clicked closed behind them. Two female heads turned to see Dr. Michael. He was tall—6'3" at least, with thick, dark hair, lightly peppered with silver, and warm brown eyes. He was broad and strong and fit.

Lynda's body tingled with an awareness of him that took her completely by surprise. Her heart was beating faster and her skin suddenly seemed more sensitive to the very air around it. Before she could stop herself, Lynda leaned toward Maddie and whispered, "You didn't mention your doctor was hot."

Maddie giggled. "Mrs. B., he's a little old for me."

He couldn't take his eyes off Lynda, even as he reached out his hand toward Maddie and shook hers. Finding his voice at last—and what a deep, rich voice it was—he said to Lynda, "Hello, I'm Michael Cameron, Maddie's doctor." He looked like he hadn't been so struck by a woman in a long time.

Lynda shook his hand. It was warm and enveloping. The air in the room was crackling with the energy between them. Her skin tingled at his touch. "Nice to meet you, Doctor. I'm Lynda Blake, a friend of Maddie's." Her voice was more breathless than she would have liked, she had to force herself to concentrate on Maddie. She was here for Maddie.

"Please call me Michael." He forced himself to let go of Lynda's hand and he went to sit behind his desk. Never had he been more grateful for a desk to sit behind. He focused on Maddie now. It was time to get focused on what was important. "Maddie do you feel like you truly understand all of your options?"

Maddie nodded silently, indicating that she did. Lynda took all the papers for Maddie, the counseling referrals. Lynda asked all the questions about who pays for the counseling, about what side effects to expect from the Plan B drugs and which ones to be worried about, what to expect psychologically in the days and weeks to come. She jotted down some notes on the papers. Maddie sat mute.

When the doctor asked her if she was ready to make a final decision, she nodded. "I'm sure, Dr. Michael. As hard as this is, it is easier than having an abortion somehow."

"And safer," Dr. Michael added, "I am glad that it was an option available to you. The drugs will start your period but the bleeding may be quite heavy. You can expect intense cramping, so be sure to get the prescription for the painkillers filled. Also remember once you take the Plan B drugs you have to lie down for at least two hours. "

Lynda squeezed Maddie's hand and smiled sympathetically.

After giving Maddie the required medication and prescriptions, Michael smiled sadly at Lynda. Her eyes locked with his. He opened his mouth to speak but before he could utter a sound Maddie turned to Lynda with a sad determined look on her face. She was ready to go. They stood up and Lynda hugged her tight. She didn't really hug back. Maddie's eyes were red and she was trying hard not to cry. Without looking up she whispered, "Thank you, Dr. Cameron."

"I'll see you soon, Maddie."

She nodded.

"C'mon, sweetheart, let me take you to the pharmacy then home." Lynda quietly ushered Maddie out of the back door of the clinic and to her car. "Let me have the keys, Maddie."

Maddie fished out her keys and handed them over. She seemed to be on automatic pilot. Lynda unlocked the car and helped Maddie into the passenger side. As Lynda started the car and began to drive, Maddie looked up and said, "Hey, wait a sec, what about your car?"

"Don't worry, I'll get Sean to pick me up at your place and take me to my car."

Maddie's eyes got large. She gnawed on her lower lip. "I guess that's okay. I mean, Paul's probably told him everything anyway."

Lynda glanced over at her. "Do you feel a little like Paul got away with something, like this didn't affect him nearly enough?"

"Absolutely."

"I have an idea, Maddie. It's a little harsh, but …"

"But what?" Maddie was actually animated. "I love Paul, Mrs. B., but he just doesn't get it."

Lynda smiled. "Have you ever seen the Cosby Show?"

Chapter 3

"harlotte, are you sure you're okay with this? I promise I'll be here the whole time," Lynda said, talking to the mother of five kids under the age of six who was on the other end of the phone.

"Are you kidding? I think it's a brilliant idea. What did you call it? Pulling a Cosby?" Charlotte said.

Lynda laughed. "Yeah. Remember when Theo didn't want to go to college and be 'regular people'? They turned the house into an apartment and furniture store and made him learn just how hard it is to survive on only a very little money."

"Actually, I do remember that one. Didn't Theo hire Cockroach as his agent?"

"Yeah. It was hysterical. So this is my chance to pull a Cosby on Paul. His mom cracked up when I talked to her about it. Her only regret was that it would only be for one night."

Charlotte said, "I think I'd like her. Hey, what are you going to do with Sean tonight?"

"Well ... "

"Uh-oh."

Lynda laughed. "Actually, I'm going to make him read Fast Girls by Emily

White."

"I read that a few years ago, I think. It's about the myth of the slut in American high schools, isn't it?"

"That's the one. I thought it was really powerful. Thinking about rumors and their effect on people's behavior is important. I've wanted Sean to read it for a few years but didn't know how to force his hand," Lynda said. "Besides, I want him too busy to really be much help to Paul."

"I remember when I read it how much it reminded me of Tina. She was the slut of my high school. She was a really nice girl actually but she sure dressed the part. What the book said about how the girls envied the slut's sexual freedom and experience and resented her at the same time really rang true."

"I know what you mean. It was a girl named Crystal at my school and the boys she turned down were worse than the one or two she actually dated. They were especially cruel in the things they said. I probably dated more than she did during high school and that seemed little enough to me. I was amazed at how long lasting the trauma of having been 'the slut' was for many of the girls in the study. They were each so isolated. I keep thinking that maybe if I had been a better person maybe Crystal wouldn't have had such a hard time. If I had just been a real friend to her, then maybe she wouldn't have been so alone and maybe it wouldn't have hurt as much to have so many people think she was someone she wasn't. I remember high school being like 'Lord of the Flies', and being relieved when someone else was being talked about because then it wasn't me. And I wasn't on the bottom rung of the social ladder. I never thought about the people on that bottom rung until later. Not very nice but that's how I was."

"Me too. It is ridiculous when you think about it, what people are willing to believe about someone. It truly defies logic. I wish I had been wiser too, but we had to grow up first, I guess," Charlotte said. She paused, " So what time do you want me to drop off Sarah for this little experiment with Paul?"

Lynda smiled, "Anytime after 4:00. He should be here by 3:30."

"Just what exactly does he think he's getting into?"

Lynda grinned, "Oh he thinks he's just hanging with Sean and getting a free meal or two. You should see the way he raids my refrigerator. It's a remarkable sight."

At four on the nose, Lynda's doorbell rang. Lynda looked up from her novel.

"Paul, that's for you."

"Me?" Paul and Sean answered the door to find Charlotte there grinning ear to ear with little two-month-old baby Sarah asleep in her car seat and a huge, overstuffed diaper bag on her shoulder.

"Hi, Sean," Charlotte said and turning to his friend she said, "You must be Paul." She handed Sarah to the baffled teenager and put the diaper bag on his shoulder. "The formula's inside. She's not on much of a schedule, really. She eats three to six ounces per feeding and needs a lot of burping 'cause she's a little colicky lately. Thanks! I'll be here at 4:00 p.m. tomorrow."

With that, she turned and left, waving to Lynda on her way.

"Mom!"

"Mrs. B.!"

"Yes, boys?"

Sean said, "Mom, what's going on?"

Lynda smiled mischievously.

Paul said, "Uh-oh, man, I think we're in trouble." He knew something big was coming

"We! We! I didn't do anything!" Sean said indignantly.

"True," Lynda said, "but I couldn't let this opportunity pass. Your job tonight is to read this book." She handed him Fast Girls.

"Mom …"

"Don't start. If you ever, I mean ever, disrespect a woman the way your dear friend here has, I will personally send you to your father! And as for you," she said, turning to Paul, "you seem eager to risk becoming a parent, so …"

"C'mon, Mrs. B. I know I screwed up. Really I do. I was scared."

Eyes flashing, Lynda said, "Well, how nice for you that you had the option of being a coward."

Paul looked to Sean for help. Sean shrugged his shoulders and put up his hands in defeat, taking a step backwards. He knew better than to argue with his mom when she was like this.

"Now, Paul," she continued, "I recall hearing you say on more than one occasion that you loved Maddie. Well, son, love is a verb, a choice, and you let her down when she needed you most. She had a future baby growing inside her, your baby, and if she had had the option of being a coward she never would have made it through the protesters, to make the hardest decision of her life, alone. She's talked to her mom, and your mom, and Sarah's Mom; and they and I have decided that for the next twenty-four hours you are going to parent little Sarah."

Paul's jaw slowly fell open. "My mom knows about this?"

"Yes."

"But I don't know anything about babies!"

"Neither does anyone, really, when they first have them. I'll be here for advice if you need it."

Sarah started to stir. Paul put down the car seat and the diaper bag. "Does Sarah's mom know that I have no idea how to do this?"

"Yes. Babies aren't that hard. They eat, sleep, burp, and poop. They're just exhausting and incessant. They need to be held and loved. You can do that, Paul, can't you? It's only for one day."

Sarah started to cry. Paul was stuck and he knew it.

"What do I do?" The helpless look on his face was pathetic.

Sean groaned. "Pick her up, Paul."

Paul looked at Lynda and Sean, then back to the crying Sarah, then back to Lynda and Sean. Lynda was reading her book.

Sean sighed and went to Sarah and unbuckled her from the car seat. "Here," he said, as he carefully handed the squalling baby to Paul. "Try rocking her back and forth."

"Okay. Uh, Sean, how do you know this stuff?"

"When they get short-handed at the nursery at church, I help out sometimes."

"Oh." Paul was stiff. His whole body was rigid. As he rocked her back and forth he patted Sarah's bottom. "Is it supposed to be this warm down here, Mrs. B.?"

Lynda looked up from her novel. "I think I'd better give you your first lesson in diaper changing."

As the evening progressed, Paul learned how to rock Sarah in her car seat as he prepared her formula and tested its temperature. He learned always, always, to put a burp cloth on his shoulder. He learned how to pat Sarah's back and rub her tummy to ease her gas. He learned how to hold her carefully to give her a bath. He learned how to sway his hips more fluidly to rock Sarah to sleep, which she did for only twenty to forty minutes at a time. He learned how to change her diapers. And by 11:30 he was exhausted.

"Mrs. B., when is she going to go down for the night?" Sarah was wide-awake, lying on her back on her blanket trying to grab a rattle Paul was dangling above her.

Lynda yawned. "I don't know. She'll probably go down for a couple of hours after her next feed. She only had a couple of ounces last time. So try to fill her up. The two of you can have the guest room. I'll sack out down here in case you need me."

"Do you really think I should sleep with her? I mean, what if I squish her?"

"You won't. Besides, she sleeps with Charlotte and Dave all the time. She likes being close to Charlotte. Not everybody does that, but it's what she's used to. And if she starts to wake up, you can rub her tummy without getting up yourself."

"Oh, that's a good idea."

Lynda smiled at him. "You're doing really well, you know."

Paul smiled. "Thanks. Thanks for all your help too."

"Well, it's only fair. After all, this was my idea."

Sean walked into the TV room where his mom, Paul and Sarah were. "Hey guys. I'm going to crash. I'll finish the book in the morning, okay?"

"Okay. What do you think of it so far?" Lynda asked.

"I think it is one of the saddest, scariest things I've ever read. What I don't know is what you want me to do about it."

Lynda looked up at her son. "I'm not sure I want you to do anything. I just want you to be aware and not judge based on rumor and appearances."

"But you couldn't have just told me that, could you?"

"Of course not. This will stick with you much longer." Lynda smiled.

Sean rolled his eyes, said goodnight, tickled Sarah, which made her smile, and went to bed.

By four o'clock the next afternoon Paul was utterly exhausted. When Charlotte arrived to pick up little Sarah, he was so relieved. "Hi, she's sleeping now. She had four ounces of formula about an hour ago."

Charlotte smiled at the unshaven teenager who looked as though he'd been up for a week. She, on the other hand, was freshly showered and feeling the best she had in weeks. "Thank you, Paul. You seem tired."

Nodding his head, he said, "Oh, man, I'm exhausted. Do you really have five kids?"

"Yes, I really do."

"Why?"

Charlotte laughed and Lynda snapped, "Paul!"

"Oh, it's okay, Lynda, he didn't mean it as an insult."

"I didn't, I swear. I ... I just don't see how you can have five kids. I mean, one is sooo much!"

After Charlotte and Sarah left, Paul collapsed on the couch opposite Lynda. She looked at him intently. "So, Paul, do you know why I made you do this?"

"Yeah, I think so."

Sean walked in and sat beside his exhausted friend.

"Sean, do you know why I made Paul do this?"

"Yeah, I think so, but what I'm still not sure of is why you made me read Fast Girls."

"Well, that was for your general education. But Paul, Maddie was well aware that she was growing a baby inside her, or what could have become a baby, your baby. That is what having sex leads to, and baby or not, choosing to prevent the life from becoming a baby is a huge deal."

Paul rolled his eyes. Sean glared at him, trying to warn him. Lynda's pupils narrowed instantly, her nostrils flared. "Paul, are you aware that the embryo that Maddie terminated had a heartbeat visible on ultrasound? Baby or not, it had a heart that was beating and it was growing inside her—taking a few pills to end it is not the same as taking antibiotics!"

Paul looked at her. "It had a heartbeat?"

'Yes."

"Oh."

"Is that the best you can do?"

"Ah, Mom, give him a break. He's sleep deprived," Sean pleaded.

"Ha! Sleep deprived is taking care of Sarah every day for two months!"

Paul and Sean groaned in unison.

"Man, I may never have kids!" Paul said.

Lynda smiled satisfied. "At least not until you're ready."

Paul stretched. "I have to go see Maddie. Catch you later, Sean. Bye, Mrs. B." He paused in the doorway and turned back to Lynda. "I think I better call my mom and thank her for taking care of me as a baby too."

"I'm sure she'd like that. Maybe you could let her know you'll think twice before being careless from now on?"

Paul grinned. "Now, I wouldn't want her to get her hopes up, would I?"

He rushed out the door as Lynda hurled a sofa cushion at him yelling, "Smart ass!"

Sean burst out laughing.

Chapter 4

The next day Lynda was enjoying a hot cider at Starbuck's with Shelly when a familiar deep voice said, "Lynda, hi."

The two ladies looked up to see Dr. Michael Cameron looking intently at Lynda. He was a tense, a little stiff. Shelly's smile at the dashing doctor went unnoticed.

Lynda's mind exploded with a thousand thoughts and her body was just about as busy reacting to the sight of him. She forced herself to smile normally and said, "Michael, hi. This is my friend Shelly."

He let out a breath of air he didn't know he'd been holding. "I was afraid you wouldn't remember me."

Shelly almost choked on her frappuccino trying not to laugh. "Oh, she remembers you."

"I'm sorry?" Michael half shook his head as he turned to look at Shelly.

"Oh, nothing," she said smugly in response to Lynda's glare. "Um, Lynda, I just remembered," she looked at the time on her cell phone, "I have to run. I have to pick up something for the kids. We'll have to finish catching up later." She got up to go. "It was very nice to meet you, Michael."

"A … you too."

Michael was still standing as if rooted in place. "Umm …"

Lynda laughed seeing for the first time that she wasn't the only one who was little nervous. "Michael, please sit down. It's nice to see you again."

"You too." He seemed to be still a bit tense.

"So … how's work? Are the protesters still hassling you?"

"A little. But truthfully, Susan doesn't let anything disrupt the office."

"I'll bet."

"I overheard her on the phone yesterday on her break chewing out some moving company guy. I guess she's moving again. No one, and I mean, no one gets the best of her," Michael said.

Lynda said flatly, "I bet that's true."

"I beg your pardon?"

"Nothing, sorry."

Michael smiled a little. "It's okay. Believe it or not she's my ex-wife. We used to own the clinic together." Why was he discussing Susan with Lynda? Stupid, stupid move.

"Oh."

They both paused.

"Isn't there something happier we could talk about?" Lynda said.

"Definitely." He paused. "Lynda, you really made an impression on me the other day."

"Oh," she hesitated, "Why?"

"Well, I was eavesdropping on you at the clinic when you were talking to Maddie. Oh boy, that sounds bad." He started to gush. "I mean, I didn't set out to, I just opened the door and no one heard me and it didn't seem a good time to interrupt and well …" His eyes were darting back and forth, he was shifting in his chair.

Lynda laughed warmly. "It's okay, Michael, really." She smiled at the handsome but embarrassed man in front of her.

"Um … well, what I wanted to say was I was amazed at your … counseling." He finally raised his eyes to her. "I've heard a lot of counseling and certainly given a lot, but I've never thought about it the way you did."

"Really? How could you not, in your line of work?"

Michael hesitated. "Is this too weird? I mean, talking about …"

"God," she finished for him. "No, not to me, but then I'm probably a little weird."

Michael smiled. "Maybe, but definitely good-weird. I guess I just didn't really know how to think about … God in a modern world. I've always just focused on how a woman's choice is so tied to her equality. I just figured the two ideas couldn't really be reconciled," Michael said.

"And here I was just hoping you thought I was cute!" Lynda said. She looked down and blushed. "I can't believe I just said that."

Michael leaned forward and touched her hand. Her gaze remained glued to the table. With his other hand he lifted her chin and made her grey eyes meet his.

"Lynda, I think you're mesmerizing."

"Oh!" Her cheeks went from pink to crimson.

Reluctantly, he let his hand drop from her chin.

Lynda managed a smile. Her chin tingled at his touch and she barely breathed for fear he would let go of her hand.

Michael's gaze dropped and he started to let go as he sat up, but Lynda leaned forward, gently putting her hand on his. His dark brown eyes flashed to hers.

"I …" she hesitated.

He waited.

"I'm not sure how to do this."

"Not sure how or don't want to?"

"It's been two years since my husband died, and, well …"

Michael's eyes looked so sad. He pulled back. "If you're not …"

"Oh, no," she cut him off. "I … I'm ready, I'm just a little rusty, that's all."

He leaned towards her, taking her other hand in his. "I haven't dated much since my divorce, haven't wanted to really, until I met you."

Lynda giggled. "Is this the part where you ask for my number?"

"I guess so."

"I should warn you, though …"

"Uh-oh, here it comes," he joked.

"I know where you work! So if I give you my number, you'd better call!"

Michael laughed. "Yes, ma'am!"

* * *

When Lynda returned home she heard Sean's voice in the kitchen and a girl's voice too.

Well, this is an interesting day for the Blakes, she thought to herself. "Sean, I'm home," she called.

"Hey, Mom, we're in the kitchen."

Naturally, Lynda thought, that's where the food is. She joined them in the kitchen. "Hi," she said. "I'm going to grab a bottle of water, then head to my office. I don't want to interrupt."

Sean cocked his head to one side and gave his mom a puzzled look. "Mom, this is Karen," he said.

"Hi, Mrs. Blake." Karen was a beautiful girl with bleached blond hair and piercing blue eyes, surrounded by too much eyeliner. She was wearing a pink crop-top and a mini-skirt barely wide enough to be a belt. It seems that Sean took his reading to heart. She wasn't sure how she felt about that, but she knew she ought to trust him.

"Hi, Karen." Lynda reached out to shake her hand. "I trust Sean is being a proper host."

Karen laughed. "Yes, ma'am."

"Please, Karen, all of Sean's friends call me Mrs. B." Lynda looked at the kitchen table; it was covered with books, photocopies, and notes. "What are you guys working on?"

"Now, that's more like the nosey Mom I'm used to," Sean laughed. "We have to do a project for our marketing class."

Lynda arched her eyebrow at her son. "Well, since you're used to my being so nosy, why don't you fill me in a little?"

Karen looked from one to the other. Sean and his Mom looked so comfortable together. Sean grinned. "Gee, Mom, we're really busy. Why don't I fill you in later?"

"I'm going, I'm going," Lynda said, holding up her arms in mock surrender. "Contrary to popular belief, I can take a hint." She turned to Karen and smiled. "It was nice to meet you, Karen. Good luck with the project, you guys. You know where I'll be if you need anything."

Karen turned to Sean after Lynda had left. "Is your mom always that cool?"

"Of course not."

"She seems really nice."

"Yeah, she's okay."

Karen looked at Sean. "You don't get it. Moms are never nice to me. Hell, for that matter guys are never nice to me unless they want something."

Sean looked right at her. "Do you think I want something?"

"I don't know yet."

He smiled. "You're very honest. I like that. Let's just get back to work, okay? We have a lot to do."

In her office, curled up on her chair, Lynda was dying to pick up the phone to call Shelly. Today was definitely a good day, hopefully the first of many.

Chapter 5

Maddie had asked Lynda to accompany her to the follow up appointment and Lynda had readily agreed. In truth she didn't want to examine her eagerness too closely. Lynda was delighted when she picked Maddie up to see that Paul was there too. They drove quietly to the clinic. When they got there Paul was stunned by the commotion out front. People were everywhere, holding placards and shouting slogans. There were pictures of fetuses and women crying.

"What is going on?"

Lynda arched her eyebrows in response. "What does it look like? This is Ron Thompson and his protestors. The very same people we had to wade through last time"

Paul looked from Lynda to Maddie. "Oh Maddie I'm so sorry I wasn't here. I should've been here with you."

She squeezed his hand. "You're here now."

When they were out of the car Paul wrapped his arms around Maddie, almost crushing her to him as they walked forward. Lynda couldn't help but smile at his protectiveness. The pro-lifers spotted them and started to swarm. Lynda turned to Maddie and Paul; "I'll distract these guys a little and meet you inside, okay?"

"Are you going to be okay Mrs. B?" Paul asked.

She nodded, "I'll be fine. This is just a war of words. You take care of Maddie."

Paul and Maddie skirted the perimeter of the protestors while Lynda headed right into the centre. Ron Thompson was giving an interview to a harried looking man jotting down notes. As the protestors tried to surround Paul and Maddie, Lynda sent up a silent prayer for courage and the right words. She took a deep breath and called out in booming voice, "Ron Thompson you should be ashamed of yourself. How can you call yourself a Christian?"

The crowd stilled instantly and turned to watch the drama unfolding before them. Ron grinned at the reporter. He turned to Lynda and swept his arms wide. "We are all here doing God's work, good lady."

"I know you believe that and you claim to be a Christian, but did you pay any attention to the New Testament? To Christ's methods?"

Ron laughed. "He worked in his time and I work in mine."

Lynda shook her head dramatically, "But Ron you are acting so righteous and condescending. These are not the characteristics applauded by Christ. He spent his time treating people with compassion and respect even when they disagreed. Why can't you do that? Why can't you be here without harassing the patients?"

"Because, my good lady, the patients coming here may already be beyond my reach. However, others who are undecided may think twice about coming because we're here. We can reach those who read about us and see us on TV."

"But you are scaring them away, not changing the way they think. That isn't reaching people; it is creating desperate situations. The whole reason God sent Jesus to us in the first place was to show us that how we live is at least as important as what we believe." Out of the corner of her eye Lynda saw the clinic door close. Paul and Maddie were safely inside. Lynda turned to the reporter. "I am a Christian too and I am pro-choice, and there are a lot of people like me in this country. We get under-reported and anti-choice activists get over-reported. Please think about that." She nodded at Ron Thompson whose eyes burned in anger, betraying an emotion his voice and body language would not. Lynda turned and walked away unmolested to the clinic door and entered the waiting room to a round of applause.

Susan walked up to her and said with genuine respect, "Wow that was amazing. I've never seen anyone stand up to him like that."

Lynda blushed, "Thanks. I figured I had a better chance of scoring points with the reporter if I didn't battle with him about the merits of his opinions rather focused on his behavior. But it was hard."

Susan held out her hand and shook Lynda's hand firmly. "Nice job."

Lynda smiled. She felt like every muscle in her body was wound up tight and she was happy for the chance to sit down and exhale.

A few minutes later, just as Maddie was called for her appointment, the door to the clinic opened again. In walked the reporter. He stood there in khaki pants and a white buttoned down shirt, holding a pad and pen and looking incredibly nondescript. He scanned the room until his eyes rested on Lynda. He nodded to her and walked over to where she stood beside Maddie and Paul.

"May I have a moment or two of your time?"

Lynda looked him straight in the eye. She tried to read him, to figure out what kind of a person he was. His eyes were blue and clear and intelligent, but guarded. She started to say no but Maddie jumped in. "No it's okay Mrs. B, go ahead. Paul's with me and you'll probably do more good out here."

"You're sure?"

Maddie nodded and Carol led Maddie and Paul back for her appointment. Lynda turned back to the reporter who pointed to a couple of empty seats for them to sit on. Lynda perched on her chair, muscles tense, ready to bolt if things went bad.

"Let me introduce myself," the reporter in his late twenties said, extending his right hand. "I am Bruce Boxter from the Merc."

Lynda shook his hand silently. His name meant nothing to her. She suddenly wished she hadn't cancelled her subscription to the San Jose Mercury News but she had never made the time to read it. "Do you have a card?"

He dug one out for her.

"Do you write for any other publications?"

"A few when I can, but nothing religious if that's what you're concerned about."

Lynda half smiled, chagrinned. "Sorry, I guess I'm kind of transparent at times."

Bruce smiled for the first time, mischief filling his face. "No problem, it makes my job easier. So ..." leaning toward her and slightly lowering his voice he said, "Will you give me what I need to make this piece a truly devastating blow to old Ron out there and his followers."

Lynda blinked in surprise at his bluntness. "Are you serious?"

"C'mon," he encouraged her, "We might just have a chance to take the Christian out of the religious right. Help me, please."

Lynda studied Bruce closely. He looked serious. It was a tempting offer despite the futility of the exercise.

"What exactly do you want from me, Bruce?"

He smiled again, she'd said his name and that was a good sign. "How about your name for starters."

"Lynda."

"Lynda ...?"

"How about we just leave it at Lynda B?"

"Okay. Can I get your phone number just so that the Merc can fact check the article before it goes to press? It won't be released, I promise."

Reluctantly Lynda gave him her cell number. He wrote it down quickly. "Okay," he said, "let's get right to it. You said you were Christian and Pro-Choice, tell me why."

Lynda found she had no problem going on record about God loving, respecting and valuing women or about the economic and political reality that equality for all women was tied to choice. The lack of choice did not prevent abortions from happening, but rather condemned women to horrifying and dangerous practices. And that allowing such barbarism in modern society was tantamount to cruel and unusual punishment as far as she was concerned.

When Lynda paused for breath, she thought about what she had just said. There was nothing she'd said that anyone who knew her would be surprised at. She just prayed that Bruce wouldn't spin it in some negative way. She looked at Bruce again.

"Wow," he said, "This is great stuff. Anything else?"

"Like free will?"

He nodded encouragingly; indicating she should keep talking. She told him more or less what she had told Maddie a few days earlier.

"Brilliant!" He said when she had finished.

Lynda sighed. She doubted very much that she'd been brilliant or even eloquent, but in for a penny in for a pound. Just then, Maddie and Paul returned to the lobby. Paul was holding Maddie's hand and some brochures. They looked over at Lynda and Bruce. Paul motioned his head to the side, questioning if she was ready to go. She nodded in response and rose to leave. Bruce got up too and shook Lynda's hand.

"Thank you so much for your time."

Lynda gave him a cold hard stare, "Don't make me regret it, Bruce."

"I won't," he said seriously. "Have you ever heard of the Christian Alliance? I'm a member of the local chapter."

Lynda had heard of the Christian Alliance. It was grass roots organization of Christians dedicated to getting religious agendas out of politics and public policy. She had in fact been an uninvolved member herself for a couple of years now, doing nothing more that writing a check once a year. Lynda smiled at Bruce now. "Good to know," she said.

That night when Sean came home he looked at his Mom across the kitchen table. "So I hear you're going to be famous?"

"I beg your pardon?"

"Your big interview? Paul told me all about it."

"Oh so Paul's been talking about me, has he?"

"Un-huh. He said you really had it out with some Lifer."

"He's exaggerating I'm sure. I just hope I get accurately represented."

Sean looked at his Mom curiously. She wasn't exactly bubbling forth with details. "C'mon Mom. Spill. What was it like being interviewed and taking on that Ron guy? It sounded cool."

Lynda sighed. "It was, kind of, and scary too. The truth is I just kind of jumped in before I thought it through, you know what I mean?" She took a bite of food and before she could continue, Sean said, "Actually I do. Paul's been giving me kind of a hard time about Karen."

Lynda raised her eyebrows in surprise. Where was this going she wondered?

"He thinks, well who cares what he thinks," Sean said trying to convince himself, "The problem is I'm not sure what I think."

Lynda racked her brain for something to say that would keep him talking. She settled on, "Mmm."

A silence loomed at the table as Sean stuffed his mouth. Lynda gave herself a two out of ten in parenting points for this conversation. "Do you see much of her in school?"

"Yeah, I guess so."

"Do you like spending time with her?"

Sean nodded as he continued to stuff his face. "Yeah but it's a little weird."

Lynda bit her tongue to prevent herself from telling him not to talk with his mouth full. "Weird how?"

"You know, everyone has all these … expectations."

Lynda nodded supportively, "Aaah," she said.

Another silence.

"What are your expectations Sean?"

He looked at his Mom. "I guess I'm not sure," he said honestly.

She smiled at her son. "I bet it would be easier for you to figure out if Paul wasn't giving you a hard time, huh?"

"Yeah and he's not one to talk."

Lynda desperately wanted to help her son. It was so hard to be seventeen. "In the end you are the one who has to live with your reflection in the mirror."

Sean rolled his eyes. "I know that Mom. You've only told me that like a thousand times."

Lynda teased him back, "Trite but true, my dear, trite but true."

Sean groaned in response.

Chapter 6

A few days later Lynda was writing furiously in a burst of creative inspiration. She had finally figured out how to get her main character out of a sticky situation when her cell phone rang. Without checking the caller ID she answered more than a little brusquely, "What?"

"Aaah ... May I speak to Lynda please?" That familiar deep voice made Lynda kick herself.

"Oh, Michael. Hi. You sort of caught me in the middle of something." She tried to sound light but was cringing inside. Of all the times to be a bear when answering the phone, she thought.

There was a pause. "I can call you back later if you're busy." He was grateful that she recognized his voice. That had to be a good sign, right?

Forcing herself to relax, she smiled and said, "No, it's okay. I'm glad you called." The voice in her head saying, I wondered how long it would take.

Michael sighed audibly at the change in her voice. "I have been meaning to call you. I heard about what you did the other day."

Lynda's mind raced but all she could come up with was, "Oh."

"Yeah, you were really something."

Another pause as she hoped for something brilliant to say from her writer's brain, "Umm thanks."

Michael paced a little and rang his fingers through his hair trying to find the next line. "Umm," he hesitated, "I was wondering if you wanted to get together for a cup of coffee or something."

She didn't even hesitate. "Sure, sounds good."

"Great."

There was another pause. Then Lynda said, "So, when would be a good time for you?"

Michael slapped himself on the forehead. "Sorry, umm, I have a break in about an hour but that is probably too last minute. I could meet you at Starbucks or I have sometime on Wednesday around 2:00, or this weekend."

Lynda told herself to be smart, make him wait at least a couple of days. Surely that was better dating strategy than meeting him at the drop of a hat, but what the hell, she ought to leave strategy to her characters. She wanted to see him. If she met him in an hour she would only have an hour to obsess over every aspect of her wardrobe and appearance and possible topics of conversation. She wasn't sure she could handle more stress than that at the moment. "Actually, I can meet you in an hour, that works for me."

"Really? Great." Michael sounded surprised and delighted.

"So, the Starbucks on Main Street then?"

"Yeah, I'll see you there."

"Okay, see you soon," Lynda echoed. She hung up and put her cell phone down. She turned back to reread her last paragraph. Again. And again. "Oh hell, what's the use?" She gave up and put her notebook and pens away and headed to the bathroom to check her hair and make up.

After an attempt at primping and preening which she was sure made no difference what so ever, Lynda did what any self-respecting woman would do. She called her best friend. "Help, Michael called and I'm meeting him for coffee in," she checked the time, "forty-five minutes."

Shelly said, "Kind of last minute, don't you think?"

"I figured it'd give me less time to stress."

Shelly laughed. "Probably a good thing, huh. What do you need help with exactly? You're meeting the man for coffee. You're beautiful and smart and funny and all without trying. Which is why I hate you by the way. So just go, relax and have fun. And remember, he's the lucky one to be going out with you."

Lynda exhaled and smiled. "You're the best, Shell. Thanks."

"You're welcome. You will call me the minute he's gone and tell me everything, right?"

"Of course."

The two friends signed off and Lynda headed down to Main Street. A little retail therapy never hurt anyone and it helped pass the time. Lynda bought herself two crystal votive candleholders that had been calling to her for months. She had always wanted to treat herself to the whole luxurious bath thing with scented oils and candles but for some reason she'd never gotten around to having candles in the bathroom. Within five minutes of the appointed hour she presented herself at Starbucks, hoping that Michael wouldn't be late because at the moment time was moving very slowly indeed.

She need not have worried. He was already there. He saw her before she saw him. He watched her exhale and smooth her hair before she entered the coffee shop. He watched as she scanned the room for him, drinking her in for a moment before he waved to her and said, "Lynda, hi. What can I get you?"

Wow, he was early. Lynda was relieved. She smiled at the sight of him. This man affected her, even from across the room. She felt alive and alert. Her nerves tingled, whether in response or in anticipation she wasn't sure. "Umm, a Grande Cider please," she answered the question at hand.

Michael nodded and forced himself to focus on ordering because if he stared at her any longer he was afraid his brain would stop functioning completely. It wasn't just the way she looked. Sure, he'd met women more beautiful than Lynda, but there was something about her, some inner beauty that made her glow. He was drawn to her.

It was a crisp, bright fall day so they decided to enjoy the air and sit outside as they sipped their drinks. They smiled at each other, not quite knowing what to say. Begin with a compliment, Michael told himself.

"You look really beautiful today."

Lynda cocked her head sideways and looked at him as if he were slightly odd. "Thanks," she replied automatically.

This made him chuckle. "You don't believe me?"

Lynda arched her eyebrows and gave him a look that said, well no.

Michael laughed out loud. "You are beautiful Lynda, believe me."

She looked down at her clothes. They were nice, comfy writing clothes; jeans, a sleeveless purple knit top covered with a shirt that had blues, purples and reds in it. Her clothes were modest but nothing special. She looked back at Michael, he was serious about his compliment and he was watching her closely, amused by her it seemed. She looked right into his deep, dark eyes and his amusement faded. She felt it now. She sat straighter and smoothed her bangs away from her eyes. She felt beautiful. The way he looked at her made her feel a lot of things. She blushed a little and looked away. "Thank you," she said again, seriously this time.

"You are welcome."

Lynda took a sip of her cider and leaned back in her chair. She needed air. "So how's work?" she said. "Are the protestors still protesting?"

From there they let the conversation flow easily on safe topics like his work at the clinic and her writing. Michael loved watching her talk about her book. Lynda's whole body conveyed her passion about her writing. She moved her arms and hands animatedly, her voice warmed as she laughed about her frustrations with one of her characters, or a stubborn sub plot that threatened to take over. At one point he wasn't even sure he was hearing what she was saying, he was so wrapped up in watching her.

Lynda finally said, "Oh I'm sorry Michael. You shouldn't get me started when I'm still working out the story. I can really blather on." She wasn't really embarrassed as such, this is who she was, take it or leave it.

"Lynda you can blather on at me any time. You clearly love what you do."

"I do," said honestly. "I really do." Lynda checked her cell phone for the time. "Oh my gosh! Michael it's already 3:30. When do you have to get back to the office?"

Michael sat up in shock. They'd been talking for over an hour! "Uh, I'd better go."

One look at him and she knew he was late. She grimaced slightly, "You're late, I'm sorry. I shouldn't have carried on so. Go."

Michael stood up and stepped towards her. He tilted her chin up with his hand and kissed her lightly on the lips. "I've enjoyed every minute. But I do have to go."

Lynda sat there as he turned to go and put her fingers to her lips where they tingled from his kiss. She felt unfamiliar warmth between her thighs. He turned back to her and said, "May I call you again?"

She nodded, lowering her hand from her mouth. He couldn't resist. He kissed her again, swiftly and deliberately. "Good," he said a second later, his eyes dancing.

Lynda laughed, "Go!"

He laughed too and went back to work with a spring in his step that he barely recognized as his own.

Two days later, Sean came upon an unusual sight in the foyer at school during lunch. Paul, Maddie and Karen were huddled together reading the newspaper.

"Sean, man, get over here, you gotta read this!" Paul said.

"Man I can barely believe my eyes, Paul are you actually staying current with the news?" Sean practically guffawed.

"Oh shut up!" Paul said.

Maddie jumped in and said, "Yeah Sean, shut up would ya. After all he's reading about your Mom."

"No way? She never told me the article was coming out today."

Karen finished reading the article and looked up. "Wow, it's really something. I think she'll be psyched at how it came out." She handed the article over to Sean.

He scanned it quickly, looking for her quotes and the overall tone of the article. "At least it sounds like her, a little more emphatic maybe but it isn't totally distorted like she was afraid it would be."

Maddie grinned, "I bet she'll be thrilled. Man, all those stats in there about domestic terrorism on clinics are killer."

Paul groaned at her choice of words.

Karen said, "Do you guys think it'll make any difference?"

"Who knows," Sean said, "It might." He paused. "Gee I hope this doesn't screw things up for Mom at church."

Maddie looked up at him. "Why would it? You guys go to the Episcopal Church don't you? Isn't it pretty liberal?"

Sean shrugged. "Yeah but … I mean it is but it's quiet about it. There is a bunch of more conservative people in it, too. And Mom still runs the preschool

Sunday school program. They might not be all that comfortable with someone so outspoken on such a controversial issue teaching the kids. I doubt Rev. John cares, he knows my Mom, but he has to answer to the congregation as a whole." He stopped there.

At Paul's dubious look, Karen said, "And isn't this whole thing about how an extreme vocal minority is disproportionately powerful with respect to a quiet reasonable majority?"

Three sets of eyes turned to look at her. Sean said, "God, I love it when you talk like that."

"Like what?"

"Like the beautiful intelligent woman that you are." He bent down and kissed her proprietarily and she blushed in response.

As it turned out Sean's concerns weren't far off the mark. When he and Karen got home after school, Rev. John was in the kitchen having tea with Lynda. Neither one of them looked happy. On seeing Sean and Karen, Rev. John Small turned to Lynda and said, "Well I guess I'd better go. I'm sorry, Lynda."

Lynda smiled and got up from the table at the same time as he did. When she spoke, her voice was strong and calm. "Honestly John, don't worry about it. You need to pick your battles and this doesn't need to be one of them. I don't mind stepping back from Sunday school."

John shook his head. "But you shouldn't have to."

Lynda nodded her head in assent but said, "It's my choice John. The Sunday school program is more important than a public show of support for my right to my personal beliefs. This just isn't the time for this fight in our congregation. Let me step back, I'm not walking away from the church and that will generate good dialogue in and of itself. That's enough. As for the rest of it, I'll be fine. I kind of have a lot going on right now anyway."

Sean and Karen silently watched this exchange. Karen reached her hand out to Sean, to touch his shoulder, to calm him. Every muscle in his body was tense; his anger radiated from him, all the more powerful for his silence, his stillness.

John turned to Sean and Karen. He looked Sean in the eye. "I'm glad you're angry. Maybe if your Mom was too, this would be an easier battle to fight."

Unclenching his jaw, Sean all but spat, "What happened to fighting the good fight, Reverend?" His tone was anything but reverent.

Lynda sighed, "Sean I love you, but we need to focus on building membership with young families right now. You know that. If my presence as a Sunday school teacher and administrator takes away from that, I'm not interested in the gig."

"Mom, this isn't right."

"I agree," Rev. John said, "But it is your Mom's choice." He turned to Lynda, "The door is always open. Know that."

Lynda smiled at him once again. "I know John. I just have a gut feeling that this isn't the fight I'm supposed to be fighting right now. And I really appreciate you being honest with me about the reactions to and the repercussions from the article."

John nodded. He knew when there was nothing else to say. He made his goodbyes and left. Sean opened his mouth to argue with his mother but she raised her hand to stop him. He groaned in frustration and went to the fridge. Lynda winked at Karen and headed up to her room to escape the day for a little while at least.

About twenty minutes later the phone rang and Sean yelled up to his Mom that it was for her. A few moments later Sean and Karen heard Lynda's voice escalating in both volume and irritation.

"Hey," she shouted, "Now you just wait a damn minute. I have never pretended to be a spokesman for the Episcopal Church. You might have noticed, in fact, that my denomination is not mentioned anywhere in the article! And the curriculum for the preschoolers doesn't exactly include discussion of such controversial topics. Go look at it, you ignorant witch! It's Noah and Jonah and Jesus and love and forgiveness and compassion! Why don't you take your judgmental condemnations and share them with someone who cares!" Lynda breathed hard and shook slightly as she slammed the phone down.

"Mom?"

"Babe, let's order in tonight okay? I'm not really up to cooking."

"Mom are you okay?"

Lynda winced at the concern in his voice. She was supposed to look out for her son not the other way around. His worry weighed on her physically. She took a deep breath, faced a smile on her face and scrambled for just enough truth to tell him so he wouldn't think she was holding out and make him worry more. "Well, you know I hate losing it like that but it felt kind of good to blast someone."

Sean chuckled at that, "Okay Mom. How about Chinese?"

"Sounds fine. Karen staying?"

"Is that okay?"

"Of course. Hey make sure and order me some Kung Pao Chicken," Lynda said.

"Done."

"Oh, and some Prawns with Snow Peas."

"Anything else," Sean asked.

"Umm, how about those spicy green beans?"

Sean laughed and left to order dinner.

The next day, the parking lot in front of the clinic was much less crowded with Ron Thompson's supporters than he was used to. He had no trouble parking his SUV and there were barely enough hands to hold all the placards he brought.

"Fear not," he said to his faithful followers. "Our mission has become more difficult, it is true, but it is no less important today than it was yesterday. We must not let the damage done by one misguided Christian deter us in anyway from saving the souls of the unborn and those who carry them."

Their passion as a group was real and vocal but it could not overcome their diminished ranks. Patients were able to enter and exit the clinic more smoothly than they had in weeks. This seemed to dishearten and discourage the Lifers. Their voices grew tired and their placards heavy. Ron appeared calm and preached steadfastness but his anger simmered.

Chapter 7

ynda's room looked like a tornado had hit it. Her bed was piled with discarded clothes. She was a wreck too. Her mind couldn't let go of the fact that she had absolutely no idea how to date. She couldn't stop thinking about Michael and sex and would she know what to do, when to do it, when not to do it, and oh God her body. No one had seen her naked in a very long time and that was just fine with her and why was she thinking about being naked anyway, this was just dinner. She didn't have time for the knock she heard on her bedroom door.

"Mom?" Sean said, looking in at the mess before him.

"What, dear?" Lynda said distractedly. "I'm in here." She was in her bathroom in her robe, doing her make-up when Sean entered. Her bathroom was a disaster too. There were towels on the floor and the counter was covered with make-up, perfume, hair spray, and other mysterious girly lotions and potions.

"Mom?" Sean coughed to hide his chuckle.

"I'm running late, Sean. What is it?"

"Umm, well ..." He looked around again. "Are you okay?"

"Okay? Of course not! I'm a nervous wreck! How did I get into this? I don't know anything about dating!" She forced herself to slow down and take a deep breath. "Never mind me. What do you need, dear?"

"I was wondering if Karen could come over so we could work on our project tonight."

"Tonight? I'm not going to be here tonight."

"Mom …" he said, as only a teenager can, chastising and begging at the same time.

"Don't 'Mom' me!"

"C'mon, I swear, we'll only work on the project."

"Swear." She sighed.

"Swear."

"I don't like it, but okay."

Sean looked at her. "I don't think you get to complain. I mean, you are going out with some guy I've never even met."

"Ha ha. I'm forty-something and you're not. Besides, I'll bring him by if it'll make you feel better."

He looked at her intently. "Really?"

"Yes. After dinner, though, okay? I don't want us to miss our reservations."

"You don't have to. I mean, it might freak him out."

"Yes, but would that really be so bad?"

Sean laughed.

"Get out of here! I have to get dressed."

Putting his hands on his hips in his best mock parenting voice he said, "I'm not cleaning up this mess, young lady. You'd better take care of it yourself!"

Laughing, she said, "I will, I promise, but tomorrow, not tonight."

Lynda turned back to her discarded clothes. She had to find something to wear. She wanted to look, well, not like a Mom, and not business like but she didn't really have anything sexy to wear either. Not that she thought for sure she could pull that off. Eventually her eyes fell on a skirt she had bought a couple of years ago from Leaf and Petal, her favorite boutique in Palo Alto. It was black chiffon and fell to just below the knee. She picked it up and tried it on. Alleluia. It still fit! She dug around some more and found a slightly shimmery soft pink knit tank top that made the most of her shoulders and arms and the least of her tummy. Now she just needed to find her favorite pair of Donald J. Pliner strappy shoes. When at last she looked at herself in the mirror she was pleased enough at the image, but the outfit still wasn't quite right.

"Jewelry," she said out loud to herself. She rooted around and found a translucent pink and aqua glass pendant she'd bought for herself in Carmel a while ago. She put it on and truly smiled. The pendant was an inch by three quarters of an inch long. It was truly unique and warm and it finished her outfit perfectly. Now she was ready, or at least looked like it.

Michael had asked Lynda to meet him at the clinic so they could leave from there together to go to dinner. Lynda liked this idea because it erased the problem of whether or not to invite him in at the end of the date, which of course had been his intent.

As Lynda was walking up the steps of the Women's Clinic she realized her blunder. *Oh my God, now I have to invite Michael home to meet Sean. Well, at least we'll have a chaperone. And worse yet, what if Susan was still there?*

It wasn't until she had reached the door of the clinic that she noticed there wasn't a protester in sight. "I guess they don't work after hours," she said to herself.

Inside she saw Susan behind the counter shuffling papers. She was in another designer suit, her shiny black hair looking perfect and her make-up professional and dramatic. In response to Lynda's smile and wave which were as relaxed as she could force them to be, Susan merely arched a perfectly shaped eyebrow at her and returned to work.

Lynda shook her head to herself. "Nice," she thought.

"Hello, Susan. Is Michael here?" Lynda said, as politely as she could.

Without looking up, Susan said, "We're closed now. Do you have an appointment?"

From around the corner behind Susan a tall, smiling man appeared. "Yes, as a matter of fact, she does."

Susan turned her head sharply to look at Michael, then to Lynda. When she spoke again her voice was full of warmth that didn't reach her eyes. "Oh, oh, wonderful. You two have a good time."

This time it was Lynda who gave Susan an arched eyebrow.

"Oh, we will," Lynda, said sweetly.

Susan's eyes locked with hers but she said to Michael, who was walking around the counter to greet Lynda, "Oh, Michael, don't forget we have an early budget meeting tomorrow morning."

He said, "Don't worry, I'll be there."

"Great, because you and I have so much to do," Susan said, also sweetly.

Lynda smiled at Michael, who hadn't taken his eyes off of her.

"Nice to see you again, Susan," she said, even more sweetly.

As soon as the door to the clinic had closed behind them, Lynda couldn't contain herself any longer and she burst out laughing.

Michael looked at her sideways. "What's so funny?"

"Oh, come on, like you didn't notice?"

"Notice what?"

"That Susan isn't exactly thrilled that you're going out with me."

Michael guffawed. "That's ridiculous!" Lynda just looked at him. "She left me three years ago for some super-wealthy investment guy and hasn't looked back since. Not that I blame her entirely. I wasn't exactly the best husband to her, not even close, really."

"Well, she's looking back now."

"No way. I'm not ambitious enough for her. She even sold me her half of the clinic in the divorce to liquidate her assets so she could invest them with this guy because I wasn't going to grow the business beyond what we have now. In truth I never really treated it like a partnership but still she never bailed on the business. Whatever her flaws she's always been loyal in terms of work. I can't blame her for wanting more. She grew up living hand to mouth and hated it. I let her believe she was getting more when she married me because I thought it was the only way to get her. Without Susan I wouldn't have any business at all, she taught me a lot and I owe her. But I doubt she would ever want me back anymore than I want her. We just weren't that good together."

"Well, think what you want. I know when a woman is acting territorial. I actually think it's kind of nice that you didn't notice."

Michael opened the passenger door to his Jaguar for her. "Lynda, you look so beautiful, I can't imagine ever taking my eyes off you."

Lynda looked down and smiled as she blushed. "Thank you," she whispered.

Michael got in the car and started it up when a thought occurred to him. "You're not worried about me and Susan, are you? I mean, she left me and it hurt like hell, but in the end it was the best thing for me."

"How so?"

"Well, it made me realize that I want a very different kind of woman in my life."

Lynda looked at him. "Well, I wasn't too worried, but I'm glad to know where you stand with her. Besides, this is only a first date."

"True," he said.

Lynda leaned back in her seat. "Besides, I kind of enjoyed making Susan a little defensive."

"Oh, really?"

"Hey, no one's perfect." She paused. "And speaking of human imperfection, I'd better call my son, Sean. He has his female school partner, Karen, over tonight to work on their marketing project."

"A mother's job is never done. How old is he?" Michael asked, as she was phoning home.

"Seventeen," she said. "It's ringing. Hello Sean, how's the work going?"

She heard him say to Karen, "See, I told you she'd call to check up on us."

Lynda laughed. "So how often do I have to call tonight?"

"I don't know, Mom, how often do I have to call you?"

"I'm in public with my date."

"I'm not on a date!"

"I'll see you later."

"Mom."

"Yes, dear?"

"Are you going to bring him by?"

"Do you want me to?"

"Well, only if the date goes well, I guess."

"I'll let you know. See you later, babe. Love you."

"Me too. Bye."

Michael looked at Lynda. "Everything okay at home?"

"Yeah, except …"

"Except what?"

"Sean wants to meet you—if the date goes well, that is."

Michael's rich brown eyes got wide. "Really?"

"Yeah. I get to check out his dates, not that he's had that many, so I guess turnabout is fair play. Are you okay with that?"

"Well, yeah, I guess I am. I kind of like thinking of him looking out for you. Do you think he'll grill me?"

"Mercilessly."

"Oh, great."

Lynda laughed. "Don't worry, my big doctor-man—I'll protect you ... a little!"

Michael laughed.

Michael drove them to a popular fondue restaurant in a nearby town. The main street was lined with trees all lit up with white lights. The restaurant was decorated in an intriguing mock luxurious safari, almost faux-medieval kind of way, with rich fabric draping the walls and ceiling. The light was dim and the rooms were small. After they had been seated and the waiter had taken their order for a bottle of wine, Lynda leaned toward Michael and said, "This place is cool. Do you eat here a lot?"

"No, but a friend told me about it and I thought I'd give it a try."

Lynda looked all around and giggled. "What a gas. Check out the pewter plates."

Throughout dinner they talked and laughed and laughed and talked. By the time the chocolate dessert fondue was ready they had discussed politics, business, reality TV, books, and the fun of eavesdropping. Lynda eyed the chocolate fondue warily.

"Oh, I couldn't possibly. I'm stuffed." *I've made such a pig of myself already,* she thought.

"Oh, c'mon, Lynda. We can't let it go to waste, now, can we?" He speared a piece of strawberry and dipped it in the chocolate. As he was spinning the strawberry to catch the dribbling chocolate, it fell off his fondue fork.

Seemingly out of nowhere, the waiter appeared. "You know the rules: if you drop food in the fondue pot you have to kiss the person you're with." Then he disappeared.

Michael was still poised over the pot trying to fish out the strawberry when he looked at Lynda. His eyes were dark and yearning, but he didn't move.

Lynda longed to feel his lips on hers but he wasn't moving. She couldn't help herself, she had to dare to be brazen. She leaned towards him. "Rules are rules," she said seriously.

He smiled, leaned forward, and brushed her lips with his, pausing just long enough to memorize their softness. When he pulled back and sat down, he was eager yet a little hesitant to read her eyes.

She was slow to open them, and when she did they were smoky with desire. Her blood pounded in her veins. One kiss and she was wet and unashamed of her desire. "Good thing we didn't know about that rule earlier."

"Why?" he breathed.

"We'd never have eaten anything!" Lynda felt free and amazed at herself. It was like someone else was speaking but it was her, an important part of her that she hadn't seen in a very long time.

Michael laughed. "I hope that means I get to meet Sean tonight."

"Mmm. Afraid so," Lynda said.

After dinner they walked hand in hand back to the car. Their fingers couldn't stay still. They were exploring the shape and texture of each other's hands. Their awareness of each other was almost fevered. Lynda had to say something to break the tension before it enveloped them completely. "Thanks for dinner. I had a great time."

"Me too," Michael said. "I can't remember the last time I had so much fun."

"Me too! But are you ready to face my over-protective son?"

"As ready as I'll ever be."

They drove back to the clinic to pick up Lynda's car. Michael followed her to her house, memorizing the way in the hopes that he would get to travel it again.

Lynda walked over to his car as he parked in front of her house.

"Ready?"

Michael took a deep breath. "Why do I suddenly feel like a teenager going in to meet a girl's father, only worse?"

"Worse?"

"Yeah, worse. I bet it's easier for a girl to go out with a guy her father doesn't like than for a mom to go out with a man her son doesn't like."

She took his hands in hers. "It'll be fine."

Michael's eyes twinkled and a mischievous smile appeared on his face. "I could use a kiss for luck," he said.

Lynda chuckled. She felt confident and powerful and very much a woman. She touched his cheeks with her fingertips and ran them into his hair. She stood on her tiptoes, closed her eyes, and bent his head to hers. She just barely grazed his lips with hers.

He groaned in response, pulling her to him.

She deepened her kiss, beginning to tease and taste him with her tongue.

He lifted her up in his arms, holding her tight as he tried not to devour her on the spot. By the time she ended their kiss they were both breathing hard. He just looked at her amazed, not knowing what to say.

Lynda smiled warmly thinking to herself, guess I remember a thing or two after all.

She looked up into those deep brown eyes. "Need a minute before we go in?"

He nodded, groaned, and hugged her close. "Lynda, you are one amazing woman." She felt a little smug knowing the affect she had on him.

When they went inside they found Sean and Karen sitting on the sofa watching TV. The two teenagers were cuddled together casually. Karen's legs were draped over Sean's lap as she lay back with her head on the arm of the sofa. When she saw Lynda, she sat up. "Uh, hi, Mrs. B. I guess I'd better be going, Sean. See you later."

"You don't have to leave on my account," Lynda said. "Sean and Karen this is my friend Dr. Michael Cameron."

The teenagers said hello as Karen fussed a little with her shirt. It almost covered her midriff. Her make up was a little lighter than before. "It's getting late. I'd better go."

Sean stood up beside her. "Do you need a ride?"

"No, it's okay, I'll walk. It's not too far."

Sean just laughed. "My mom raised me better than that, Karen." Putting one hand on his hip, shaking his other index finger in the air, and mocking his mother's voice, he said, "Never, I repeat never, let a lady go home by herself after dark. A gentleman always sees to the safety of his lady friends."

Karen, Lynda, and Michael all burst out laughing.

"I do not sound like that!"

Sean rolled his eyes.

"I don't!"

"Come on, Karen. I'll take you home."

Lynda smiled; watching as her son gently put his hand on the small of Karen's back. Karen ducked her head a little shyly as he did so. Sean turned to look at Michael.

"I guess you're off the hook for now. I'll have to interrogate you another time." He winked, then ushered Karen out the door.

Hearing the door close made Lynda startle. Her eyes darted around the room. Somehow the air seemed to have left her lungs as she found herself suddenly alone with this very attractive, very large man. "Well," she said. "Here we are. Would you like some coffee or something?"

Michael shifted his weight from foot to foot. "Well, I know I don't want to say goodnight just yet."

Lynda lowered her eyes and smiled. He stepped closer to her. He leaned toward her, inhaling. "You smell wonderful."

He touched her hair with his fingers so gently, as if it were spun gold. Slowly he lowered his mouth to hers, hovering just above her lips. Lynda stood motionless, afraid to move. Her heart was pounding. At last he kissed her, gently at first, but finding no hesitation in her, he deepened his kiss, exploring her mouth completely, demanding her response, claiming his right to know her. He all but pushed her against the wall, locking his hands with hers, feeling the curves of her body pressed against him, feeling her heart pounding as hard as his. Finally he released her mouth and began to kiss her face, her cheeks, and her eyelids.

Lynda moaned, feeling her body taut with desire.

"Oh Lynda, Lynda," he murmured, as he nibbled on her ear. "What you do to me!" He paused to catch his breath, let go of her hands, and caressed her sides, finally resting his hands on her hips. His blood was pounding in his veins. He looked her in the eye and saw his own desire mirrored there. He sighed.

"I got a little carried away," he said.

"Mmm."

"Sorry."

She laughed, "No you're not!"

"Maybe not, but I am surprised at myself. I usually have great self-control."

Lynda smiled. "Well, I'd hate to be the only one needing a cold shower tonight."

"Woman, I swear you make me feel sixteen again."

"Funny, I feel more like a grown woman now than I have in a very long time."

Michael groaned in frustration.

From behind them came Sean's voice. "Ahem. Hi Mom, Dr. Cameron."

Lynda closed her eyes and moved in front of Michael screening the evidence of his desire. Opening her eyes and forcing them to meet her son's, she said, "Hi Sean. Did Karen get home okay?"

"Yes."

"Good."

With a twinkle in his eye, he looked at Michael. "I guess you're not off the hook after all. Perhaps we should begin by discussing your intentions."

Lynda gasped.

Michael started to cough but recovered. "Why don't we sit down first?"

Sean waved his arm towards the library as he followed Michael and his mom into the room. Lynda sat beside Michael on a sofa opposite Sean. Turning to Michael, she said, "Okay, now I feel sixteen."

Michael took her hand in his.

"So, Dr. Cameron ... "

"Please call me Michael."

"Okay, Michael, tell me about your intentions?"

Lynda glared desperately at her son. "Really, Sean, this is ... ", Lynda said.

Michael smiled and patted her hand. "It's okay—in for a penny, in for a pound." He looked at Sean. "My intention is to get to know your mother a whole lot better. I think she's an amazing woman."

"I see." Sean's eyes twinkled. "And what are your prospects?"

"Sean!" Lynda said, really he could be the most exasperating child.

Michael had caught the twinkle in Sean's eye and understood that the object of this exercise was mostly about making Lynda squirm.

"Well, Sean, I own my own business and it supports me in a very comfortable lifestyle. I also recently received a sizeable inheritance from my uncle."

"Oh, Michael, I'm sorry," interrupted Lynda. "When did he die?"

"About six months ago. He was sick for a long time, though; in a way, it was a blessing he finally let go."

Sean was watching his mother.

Very seriously he said, "Michael."

"Yes."

"Don't hurt her."

Michael and Lynda looked at him.

Lynda started to speak, but Michael stopped her. He looked at Sean and said, "I promise I will never deliberately hurt your mother and I will try never to hurt her at all."

Sean nodded. "Okay, then."

Chapter 8

The next day Lynda was getting her dark Irish eyebrows waxed. As she was sitting at Tosca's station in a bright modern salon in Menlo Park, her esthetician and friend, was clearly a little worried about her. She was too quiet.

"Okay, girl, give it up. What's going on with you today?" said the beautiful, African-American woman. Tosca always made it look easy to dress in well put together outfits that were chic and friendly. Lynda didn't know how she did it.

Lynda was in jeans and a t-shirt that would have looked shabby on anyone else. She sort of grinned. "Sorry, I guess I'm kind of quiet."

"Yeah, are you okay?"

Lynda smiled at her friend. She knew she could always count on Tosca for good counsel; her concern, as with everything else about her, was totally genuine.

"Actually, you're going to like this."

"Not if it makes you look the way you do today I won't."

"Well, see, there's this guy …"

"Whoa, back up! When did this happen? I just saw you last week!"

"Well, obviously I met him since last week. I'd never hold out on you, you know that."

"You better not. God knows you listen to me enough."

"The problem is that, well, we went out last night, and … "

"And … " Tosca waited with bated breath.

"And we kissed."

"All right!"

"More like made out, actually."

"Excellent! But what's the problem?"

"David," Lynda said in a word.

Tosca kept waxing Lynda's eyebrows, waiting and watching.

"I'm not sure how I thought I'd feel kissing someone else, wanting someone else, but I thought I would feel—I don't know—torn."

"How do you feel?" Tosca asked, as she started to pluck.

Lynda sighed. "I'm not sure. Not torn or guilty. I think I feel guilty for not feeling guilty! I miss David—a lot—but at the same time he's still with me too, and Michael, well, it just feels so good to feel like a woman again. I mean, wow, we're talking major STS here."

"STS?"

"Screaming thigh sweats! The man makes me want to invest in Duracell, if you know what I mean."

The two ladies burst out laughing.

"Tell me, Lynda, what would David think of Michael?"

"If I'm right about him, I'd swear David picked him out for me."

"Maybe he did."

"Maybe. Time will tell."

Tosca was smoothing some gel over Lynda's once-again-perfect eyebrows. "Keep me posted."

"I will, but hey, I didn't get a chance to find out what was going on with you."

"Everything's fine. Nothing that won't keep until next week."

"Thanks, Tosca! You're the best."

Tosca smiled. "I can't wait until to find out what's happened with Michael."

"Dr. Michael!"

"Doctor indeed. How's Sean handling it, by the way?"

"You mean after catching us making out in the hallway?"

"No way!"

"Oh yeah, he then proceeded to grill Michael about his intentions, just to make me squirm."

Tosca laughed. "He really is your son, isn't he?"

"Undoubtedly!"

The two women hugged goodbye and Lynda left Tosca's.

When Lynda got home, Sean was there with Karen and they were flipping through the channels when Lynda said, "Go back."

"What?"

"Go back to the local news."

Lynda watched as a reporter stood in front of the protesters in front of the Women's Clinic.

"What is it?" Karen asked. She hadn't missed the urgency in Lynda's tone.

"That's Michael's clinic," Lynda answered.

"Michael?"

"Mom's new boyfriend, remember?" Sean said.

"Oh yeah."

"One date does not a boyfriend make," Lynda said defensively.

"Whatever you say, Mom."

Ron Thompson was staring back at her from the TV. The supporters around him had thinned in number since her encounter with him and the quietly scathing article Bruce had published a few days earlier. When she heard Ron's voice it sent a chill down her spine. Looking straight into the camera, he said, "Despite what some people may think, I know that my mission to save the lives of unborn babies is a Holy one. No one will ever stop me from the path the Lord has chosen for me."

Lynda shivered. She felt like he was talking directly to her. She shook her head telling herself she was being ridiculous. The news clip ended without giving Lynda any information she wanted about the clinic.

Karen was wearing a tank top and tight jeans and sneakers. No midriff in sight. She was wearing still less eyeliner. She turned to Sean and said, "Hey, if this guy, Michael, owns his own business, why don't we interview him for our marketing paper? Do you think he'd mind, Mrs. B.?"

"Probably not. My guess is you'll want to interview Susan, too. She does a lot of the operations part of the business, I think. She used to be part owner of the business before they divorced."

Karen nodded. "That's a good idea. Thanks." Turning back to Sean she said, "Well, what do you think?"

Sean looked at Karen appreciatively. "I think it's a great idea. I think you are even smarter than you are beautiful."

Lynda noticed that Karen had the good grace to blush.

Lynda smiled at Sean from ear to ear. "You are just like your father! I'll see you two later." She left the TV room and headed to the kitchen to make dinner.

"Hey Karen, are you staying for dinner?" Lynda asked a few minutes later.

"You wouldn't mind?"

"Of course not. I cook for an army every night with Sean around."

Karen giggled. "Okay then, thanks." She paused. "Hey, why don't you invite Michael over and we can interview him over dinner."

"Uh, I don't know."

Karen nudged Sean. "It's okay with me, Mom," Sean said.

"I can call him and ask. I guess there's no harm in that," Lynda said, more to herself than to anyone else.

Out of earshot of Lynda, Karen turned to Sean, "So what do you want to know about this guy? Here's our chance to get all the dirt."

Sean smiled. "Actually, I already sort of grilled him the other night. Can you believe when I got home from dropping you off I caught them making out in the hallway!"

"No way!" Karen all but shouted.

Lynda poked her head in the TV room. "Everything okay in here?"

Two pairs of eyes looked at her assessingly.

"Mrs. B., I'm impressed."

"I beg your pardon?" Lynda was puzzled. Then a light dawned, she looked at her son. "Oh Sean, you didn't tell her!"

He just nodded. Lynda turned bright red and went back to the kitchen. Walking away she called back to them. "He'll be here for dinner, so be nice!"

"Yes, ma'am," two voices responded in unison.

Half an hour later, Michael rang the doorbell, shifting from foot to foot and smoothing his hair as he waited. Sean opened the door. He looked at Michael, looked at the big bouquet of flowers in his hand, and nodded, "Nice touch," he said.

"Mom! Your date's here!" he bellowed. "Come on in. She'll be down in a minute."

Michael stood in the doorway waiting. Lynda poked her head into the TV room. "I'm in ... where is he?" she asked Sean.

Sean pointed his thumb toward the entrance hallway. Walking to Michael, she gave her son the "What's the matter with you?" look. He shrugged his shoulders.

"Hi Michael, sorry about Sean's manners."

Michael presented her with the bouquet of pink and purple flowers full of lilies and freesia and pink roses. "Ooh, these are beautiful. You didn't have to!"

"Yes he did!" Sean said.

"Sean!" the two women rebuked.

Michael surveyed the scene in front of him. "Actually, Sean's right, ladies. Any self-respecting gentleman would bring flowers with him." He winked at Karen. "Remember that," he said to Sean. Then turning to Karen said, "Karen, right? Nice to see you again." He held out his hand to her. She shook it firmly but her eyes were a little wary. She forced herself to relax; he wasn't her father after all.

As Lynda finally took the bouquet Michael kissed her cheek. Lynda couldn't contain her smile. "It's nice to see you."

"Thanks for the invitation."

"Any time."

"Be careful what you wish for."

Lynda and Michael headed to the kitchen. "Dinner will be in about 15 minutes, kids," Lynda said.

In the kitchen Michael helped set the table and opened a bottle of wine. Lynda couldn't take her eyes off him. She loved the way he moved. She loved seeing the play of the muscles of his back under his shirt as he leaned over the table. While standing at the island opposite the sink, she dropped the tongs she was using to toss the salad and had herself a nice view of his slacks straining watching over his perfectly sculpted derriere.

When he turned to look at her she looked down, trying to remember what she'd been doing. He walked over and stood behind her. "Woman," he said, "if you keep looking at me like that we're not going to make it to dinner."

His warm breath on the back of her neck made her shiver with desire. Lynda smiled to herself. He had noticed her noticing him. How could her body react so strongly to this man? His very proximity made her skin tingle and when she looked into those eyes … she had no idea that she could get so excited so fast.

"I think that salad has had all the tossing it can take."

Lynda forced herself to put the salad tongs down. She wiped her hands on her new Cabrio stretch jeans, which did a lot for her butt and tucked in her little tummy. Michael put his hands on her shoulders. He turned her around. He ran his hands slowly down her side and rested them on her hips. She leaned back against the counter. Her hands found their way to the hair at the base of his skull and began massaging him gently.

Michael closed his eyes and quietly moaned in pleasure. He looked at this beautiful creature in his arms and bent his head to hers and kissed her. She knew she should be cautious. They were not exactly alone. She tried to force herself to be responsible, but every time she inhaled, his musky scent teased her. She kissed him back with a longing she didn't know she had. Her body felt so alive and sensual, it was like she was swimming in pleasure that she had thought was lost to her, if indeed she had ever really known it at all. She ran her hands down his back; pressing with her fingers so hard it almost hurt him. Finding his hips she pressed them to hers and groaned in satisfaction. She loved feeling him hot and hard and pressing against her. She was a hunter just as much as she was prey and she loved it. The power she had to excite this man, the power of her fast, wet arousal stunned Lynda and demanded to be obeyed. The pleasure she knew he would give her made her lovely nights with Duracell pale in comparison. She started to tug at his shirt when some part of her mother's brain heard footsteps approaching. She pushed Michael away quickly. He was confused and looked at her questioningly. Then two teenagers appeared just as the smoke detector blared. She'd almost got caught again! What was she thinking? Why wasn't she thinking? Why was she so damned dizzy? Lynda chastised herself profoundly. It only helped a bit that she knew she would find this amusing eventually. She dared to admit the truth to herself for a brief second; she really needed to get laid.

Karen and Sean looked at the two grown-ups breathing hard. The smoke and the smoke detector blaring finally penetrated Lynda's foggy brain. "Oh no, the garlic bread!"

Michael retucked the back of his shirt and went to open the back door to let the smoke out. Karen tugged on Sean's arm. "Come on, let's go turn off the smoke detector."

Sean just shook his head and let Karen lead him away.

A few minutes later, all four people sat at the kitchen table silently, politely eating garlic bread burned beyond recognition.

"Oh, this is inedible," Lynda said. She sighed. "Sorry, guys." She picked up all the garlic bread and threw it away. "Hopefully the lasagna and salad will be enough to fill us up."

When she sat back down Michael squeezed her hand. "This lasagna is really delicious. It's such a treat to have a home-cooked meal. Thanks."

She smiled back at him.

Michael let go of her hand and looked at Sean and Karen. "I understand I have to sing for my supper, however."

Karen pulled out her notebook and pen and said, "Thanks for letting us interview you, Dr. Cameron."

"Please call me Michael."

She paused. "Okay, Michael. Sean and I are doing a paper on marketing for small businesses, and you have an interesting business in that I can't remember seeing any ads or local TV spots for it."

"Well, it is true that it is a hard-to-market kind of business, but we do try to quietly make our presence known. For instance, I am in regular contact with local doctors, nurses, hospitals, and guidance counselors, and I always leave them pamphlets and cards. Also, our location was chosen specifically for its visibility and our signage is prominent. But traditional PR doesn't work for us. It is expensive and, frankly, reasonableness doesn't sell well on the news."

Karen was busily taking notes. Sean swallowed a big bite of lasagna and said, "What do you mean, reasonableness doesn't sell?"

Michael held up one finger begging for patience as he finished a bite of food. He wiped his mouth and said, "The press doesn't report about our work preventing unplanned pregnancies through education and contraception. They don't report on our counseling programs that follow up with our patients months and longer, if necessary, after they have terminated their pregnancies. Or our counseling about all the options available to our patients, including giving up a child for adoption and helping people throughout that process and afterward. The news doesn't report that we make sure the people who choose to keep their babies get proper care during and after their pregnancy, including helping them begin to navigate the social services available to them. Or any of the other care we provide for women suffering from infertility, depression or menopause and so much more; or that not surprisingly most of our patients are low income. These things are all perfectly reasonable. It makes common sense that we should provide all of these services, but the media only cares that we perform abortions. It's really frustrating, actually."

Karen was furiously writing, and when she finished she looked up. "How do you feel about the sound byte on the news today?"

"About the protesters, you mean?"

Karen nodded.

"Frankly, it infuriates me. Susan, our VP of Operations and office manager disagrees. She says there is no such thing as bad press; at least people will know we're here. But I disagree. The news makes light of the harm the protesters cause, discouraging—even preventing—people from getting the medical and psychological treatment they need. Also, the anti-choicers make the issue of access to safe and legal abortions about the life and death of the baby, but the truth is, it is about the life and well being of the woman who is pregnant. It wasn't that long ago really where coat hangers were still something women had to worry about. And while this country purports to be tough on terrorism, they exclude the domestic terrorism of the religious right, to which most, if not all, of these protesting organizations have links. Do you have any idea how expensive my liability and property insurance rates are compared to other similarly sized medical practices? The insurance companies take the terrorists seriously but no one else does. There is nothing the police can do about the letters and the phone calls until something big happens. California's been pretty safe, but these news blurbs bring out the whackos. Just you wait: before too long I'll be back to screening all my calls and having the post office hold my mail."

Lynda arched an eyebrow at this. "Should I be worried?"

Michael sighed. "No, I don't think so. I mean, nothing has ever happened to me besides the phone calls and letters. It's more the general disruption of my life, my staff's, and my patients' that infuriates me. I heard a quote on a Law & Order rerun last night: 'Sometimes the good you do does you no good at all.' That's how I feel sometimes. Sorry, guys, I guess I'm ranting."

Sean said, "No, it's okay. You gave us some great stuff. Thanks for being so candid with us."

"Until recently I hadn't thought what I do, and God, could coexist happily. But now that I do, the anti-choicer's use of God to keep women down infuriates me even more."

After dinner Sean and Michael cleared the dishes from the table and Lynda and Karen chatted.

"Michael seems like a good guy," Karen said.

"Thanks. I like the way he jumps in and helps out."

"I like the way he doesn't B.S. He just tells it how it is."

"Now, I just have to figure out what his flaws are and whether or not I can live with them."

Karen thought about that for a moment. "That's an interesting way to look at it, Mrs. B."

"I learned a long time ago that people don't change unless they want to. If you're going to choose to love someone, that means accepting them as they are, and knowing it may never get any better."

Karen looked over at Sean. Conspiratorially she said, "I don't suppose you'd like to fill me in on Sean's flaws, would you?"

Lynda laughed.

Hearing the mirth, Michael said, "Uh oh, they are definitely talking about us."

"Don't tell me you're surprised!"

Chapter 9

Lynda had started a fire in the living room fireplace. She was in one of her favorite rooms. She loved the built-in bookcases lining two walls that were filled to bursting with her, David's, and Sean's books. She loved the piano in the corner that David had taught himself to play, and that Sean still tried from time to time. She loved the rich green sofas that were great for curling up in and the Oriental rug she and David had picked out. And now here she was with Michael. Dr. Michael Cameron, who had waltzed into her life and her son's. They were sitting together with Lynda's legs draped over his, as she leaned with her back on the arm of the sofa. She bit her lip in worry and sat up.

"What is it, Lynda?" he asked, concerned.

"I ..." she sighed, "I'm worried that I did the wrong thing introducing you to Sean right away. I mean, it's against all the rules, isn't it?" She started to get up, then decided against it.

Michael's eyes darted back and forth. He didn't know what to say. "I thought ... I mean, here I thought I was doing so well." He sounded distraught.

"You are, you are," she reassured him, absently patting his thigh. She was really talking with her hands now, he knew that couldn't be a good sign. "It's just that

I don't know what's wrong with you yet, and you don't know what's wrong with me."

Michael looked at her. "You're stressing because I haven't done anything wrong?"

"Yes. And, well, how do I know if you'll still like me once you see all my flaws? There are a lot, you know."

"You mean like being a little neurotic from time to time?"

"Exactly," she said, ignoring the twinkle in his eye.

"So you would feel better if I gave you a list of my flaws, to the best of my knowledge?"

She nodded sheepishly.

He chuckled a little nervously. "I guess you don't like to waste your time. Okay, then." He took a deep breath. "I took a long time to grow up and realize that life is about real connections with other people not just about me. I can be very stubborn, even arrogant. I like to learn from my own experiences, not other people—I am trying to work on that one. It's cost me a lot of time. I like that I'm reasonably attractive. Should I keep going?"

"Could you?" Lynda asked. She paused. "Do you lie?"

Michael smiled. "Very badly."

Lynda smiled. "I believe you."

Michael wrapped his arms around her as she snuggled back into him. "And you? What are your major character flaws, Mrs. B.?"

She giggled. "Besides being a little neurotic from time to time?"

"Mm hmm." He nuzzled her hair.

Focus, she told herself, he asked you a question. "Well, I'm very stubborn. I can be arrogant, thinking others need me to help them sort out their problems." The warmth of his breath on her ear made her shiver. "I get insecure from time to time. I have an Irish temper. I think computers have little gremlins in them." Her voice began to quiver, but the longer she could pretend to ignore him the longer he would tease her. "Mmm, I love The Bold and the Beautiful. I am too decisive; I rush to decisions to avoid uncertainty. I am working on that one, sort of …" Her breathing was getting shallow and her pulse quickened. This man made her really understand that skin was an organ, a very sexual one at that.

Michael continued to nuzzle her hair and began to lightly caress her arms.

"Mmm … where was I?" Her whole body hummed in awareness of him and of itself. She wanted where this was going. She wanted to be unable to resist the call to pleasure building inside of her.

Michael started nuzzling her ear. "I haven't run screaming from the room yet, but then I don't know what The Bold and the Beautiful is." He kissed behind her ear and slowly trailed kisses down her neck.

She sighed, and somewhat amazed at her own coherence she actually was able to answer his question. "Umm, it's a TV soap opera. My guilty pleasure."

"Maybe I could expand your repertoire of guilty pleasures," he whispered.

"Mmm, maybe you could." Now we're talking, she thought. He felt so safe, strong and safe. She knew that it was okay for her to be with this man, knew that she would discover new things about herself with him.

Michael ran his fingertips along the top of her hands, her wrists, her arms, barely kissing her breasts with his touch as his fingertips worked their way up to her shoulder, and there he paused.

"Lynda …"

Something in his voice made her turn to look at him. Don't break the mood she silently begged.

"You're not going to run screaming from the room when you realize I am all the things I told you about, are you?"

She raised her hand to his handsome face, looked him straight in the eye and said, "No, I think I can handle you just fine."

He exhaled. "Good."

"Yeah, good."

She ran her thumbs over his eyebrows slowly. She put feather kisses on his eyelids, as she straddled him with her legs. She kissed him, giving him herself, knowing it was too soon, knowing it was too fast, knowing she didn't care about anything at that moment but giving this wonderful man her heart.

Michael felt his heart begin to race. His blood was pounding in his ears. He was dizzy. He felt her demand to love her in her kiss. He knew that, if he didn't stop now, it would be too late.

Michael pulled back gently. Man nobility sucks, he thought. He took Lynda's face in his hands, holding it as if it were the most exquisite fragile crystal in the world. Looking deep in her eyes, he said, "Lynda, sweet Lynda." He gently brushed her lips with his. "You make me want to absorb you. You are pure light."

She searched his eyes silently.

"You said you are too decisive. Are you being too decisive now? I don't want you to regret anything."

Lynda sat back on her heels. Her mind raced. Didn't he want her? Maybe he did, but he didn't want to love her? Maybe she was confusing lust and love. But no, that wasn't it. Watching him with Sean and Karen, seeing him as a doctor with Maddie, this man had a spirit worth loving, and …

"Michael, if you don't want to love me, let me know now." She watched him, waiting for his reaction.

"Oh Lynda, I do want to l … love you, but I just don't know. It's so fast."

She smiled. "You tripped on the l-word."

Nodding, he said sheepishly, "Yes, I mean, I've been married before but I'm not sure I know much about love, not really."

"Well, I have loved well and been well loved …"

"Hey, I am not sure I want to think about you being well loved by someone else!"

Tapping his nose with her finger she said, "You're cute when you're jealous. As I was saying, I do know something about love, and it's a leap of faith, a choice you make every day. Are you willing to let me see you at your worst, let me be there for you, and vice versa?"

"That's huge, Lynda. No one has ever been there for me. I've had to count on myself."

She smiled like a beautiful sage of old and said, "Well, that's the journey we're on. If you want to keep going, follow me." Lynda looked so brazen and bold as she got up off the couch, turned her back on Michael, and left the room. Never had her ears strained so hard to hear every little noise. She must be a lunatic, she told herself. Nobody in their right minds moved this fast but hell, when you know, you know. Why fight it and waste time? She really ought to read Dating For Dummies, she thought. Her mind was going a zillion miles a second.

She was about to turn the corner and head upstairs when she paused, still waiting for a sound, a creak, anything! Just as she began to feel really foolish, as her head began to fill with recriminations, she had rushed him ridiculously after all, the sofa creaked. Worried about which way Michael would turn—toward the door and out of her life or toward her and right into the center of it—she turned to look at him over her shoulder.

Michael went to the entryway and looked at the mystical woman before him. She smiled a happy, knowing smile. He was hers.

Michael hesitated for a moment, but followed quietly. On the landing, before he turned to climb the final set of stairs, he heard two voices talking and laughing behind closed doors. He was stunned. He looked at Lynda and saw the horror on her face. They had actually forgotten all about Sean and Karen! He took her hand and headed back down the stairs. On the landing the floor creaked lightly and Sean popped his head out of his room expecting to see his Mom coming up to check on him.

"Mom," he said accusingly.

Lynda's faced flushed, "I was just giving Michael a tour."

"Uh huh." Sean was clearly unimpressed. Michael's eyes darted between the two of them. He didn't want to be in the middle of this or to come between them.

Michael let go of Lynda's hand and edged away from her. Lynda turned to Michael; "I'll meet you in the library." It was an order he didn't dare question.

He nodded, happy for the escape.

Lynda and Sean just stood there staring at each other silently. The air was as charged as a summer electrical storm. Finally Lynda sighed and lowered her eyes momentarily.

"Look Sean," she began.

He folded his arms across his chest and leaned on the doorframe of his bedroom door. He was not unaware of how to make himself physically imposing. Karen stayed discreetly hidden in his room. With his voice dripping with superiority, he said, "Yes."

Lynda was frustrated and testy. God wasn't it hard enough to consider having sex again after all this time without having Sean make it more difficult. I mean good Lord she was actually going to let Michael see her naked! But that was the price she had to pay for getting some pretty basic needs met. "Gee thanks for making this easy for me."

"Making what easy for you?" The condescension in his voice washed over her like a cold rain.

"Don't be such an ass." Her patience had expired. "Call Paul and stay over at his house tonight."

"Mom!" Sean's jaw dropped open. He couldn't believe his ears.

"Do it," Lynda commanded. She turned on her heel and went downstairs to the library.

When Michael saw her he was a little afraid that she might snap into pieces, she was so tense. "Are you okay?"

Lynda waved her hand in the air. "Oh who knows?" She plopped herself down on the sofa and held her head in her hands. Michael sat beside her and she immediately got up and started pacing. He just watched her move like a caged animal. Even agitated she had an incredible grace to her movements, one he was sure she was completely unaware of.

"Oh God, I hate screwing up as a parent. I mean I know it'll be okay but still I'm supposed to get it right." Her words were rushed and harsh.

"Sean is a great kid. You're obviously doing something right."

Still pacing Lynda laughed self-deprecatingly, "Ha! All that means is that I haven't ruined him yet! I just put my needs over my kids needs and that's bad!"

"No Lynda it's not. Sometimes you have to put yourself first otherwise you won't end up on the list at all."

She turned to look at Michael, really look at Michael.

He shrugged, "I meet a lot of Moms in my line of work, trust me on this one."

She did. What he said had a ring of truth to it. Finally she sat beside him on the sofa and bumped her shoulder against his. "Still, it's not one of my better moments."

Michael put his arm around her. "I can go Lynda. Honest it's okay."

Lynda opened her mouth to respond when they heard two pairs of footsteps, one all but stomping down the stairs. Sean soon faced his mother in the library. His back was ramrod straight and he held Karen's hand in a death grip. "I'm taking Karen home then going over to Paul's."

Lynda nodded but said nothing.

Karen's eyes took in the scene before her and she said, "Good night Mrs. B, thanks for dinner. Good night Michael." She tried not to smile but she seemed rather amused by the whole thing.

"Good night Karen," Lynda said ignoring Karen's suppressed mirth. "I'm sorry about … the way the evening ended." The look of complete desolation on Lynda's face was just too much. Karen couldn't help herself and she laughed out loud. She hugged Lynda impulsively and whispered in her ear, "Have a blast Mrs. B."

Lynda was so stunned she couldn't respond. Sean shot daggers at Karen but she couldn't hide her smile.

Closing the front door behind themselves, Sean turned to Karen. "How could you encourage her like that?" Sean asked accusingly. His body was taut and large and still.

She flicked his arm with her hand and laughed. "Oh Sean, don't be so stuffy. She's been alone a long time, let her live a little."

"She's my mother!" he snapped at her.

"How do you think she got that way?" she lightheartedly shot right back.

"I don't want to think about it." He was confused. Karen's reaction was so strange. She was so calm about it all.

Karen laughed. "You're just jealous because she's gonna get some and you're not."

He paused and quietly admitted, "I never have."

"Really?"

He nodded, "Though not for lack of trying."

"You haven't tried with me."

"Yeah, but I really like you."

Karen looked at him confused. "I swear to God men don't make any sense at all. Sex is supposed to be for people who care about each other."

"It's not that simple."

"Tell me about it," she said not able to keep a deep sadness at bay. Hearing it Sean pulled her into his arms and held her close. His need to protect her drowned out every other feeling he'd ever had.

In the house, Lynda stood up and turned to Michael and said, "I, um, I'm not sure …"

He stood too and kissed her sweetly, briefly on the lips. He hugged her, meaning it to be comforting. Lynda snuggled into his arms and reveled in their strength. He stroked her hair and she sighed. He could feel the tension slowly leave her body. Before long the energy between them changed and grew charged once again. Michael caressed her back and she rested her hands on his tush. She couldn't resist squeezing it. When she looked up at him he bent his head to hers and she leaned into him pressing her body next to his. Michael ran his hands down her back and cupped her delightful derriere. He pulled her to him intimately. Lynda moaned in response. She knew what she was going to do. She didn't want to resist him or herself. Right now she didn't care about anything but this moment. Except for one thought.

"Um, do we need to make a trip to the drugstore?"

"I've got some protection with me."

With a gleam in her eye, "That was a little presumptuous, don't you think?"

Michael grinned back. "Actually, I better check and make sure they're not expired." Linda giggled. Sure enough, they were. When Michael showed Lynda the expiration date, they both cracked up. They had expired over a year ago!

On returning from the store, Lynda took Michael's hand and led him back to her bedroom. She hesitated briefly when he began to take off her shirt. He felt it and tried to kiss away her doubt. The feel of his lips on her bare skin made her quiver, but she couldn't quite relax. As Michael trailed kisses down her tummy and began to undo her pants, Lynda stilled and bit her lip. He looked up at her questioning. Lynda sat down on the bed.

"It's kind of bright in here," Lynda said. I can't possibly be ready to let him see me naked, can I? I am not exactly twenty-three anymore. Why can't I get my mind to just turn off?

Never taking his hands off of her, Michael sat beside her. He kissed her shoulder. "You are so beautiful."

Biting her lip once again Lynda reached over to the bedside table and turned down the light. The muted glow relaxed Lynda somewhat. Michael trailed kisses along her collarbone and got on his knees before her and to make his way down to the waistband of her pants yet again. This time instead of continuing to undo them, he trailed kisses over them working his way to the heart of her pleasure.

Lynda stroked her hands through Michael's thick dark hair, closed her eyes and fell back on the bed. He gently eased her out of her pants and quickly removed his own shirt. He ran his hands up her legs and massaged her inner thighs. He returned to kiss her over her panties. She was hot and wet. He moved her panties aside so he could taste her for himself.

She inhaled audibly at the first feel of his mouth on her. She covered her face with her arm to hide her face as her pleasure took control of her. He expertly teased, tasted and tormented her. Lynda grabbed the bedspread tightly in her hands as she felt the heat and tension build inside her. Her hips rocked and Michael cupped her behind and moved with her never breaking the rhythm of his intimate kisses. When she came she cried out with the force of it. She shook, the intensity of her spasms surprising them both and still he kissed her.

As she quieted, Michael kissed her thighs and began to move to join her on the bed, removing his pants as he did so. She had once again covered her face, embarrassed at herself, her reaction to him, her losing herself in her orgasm. He held Lynda and sensed that she was about to speak so he put his finger on her lips, stilling her, saying, "Shh."

She turned to look into his eyes and he kissed her eyelids. He began to make love to her again. He kissed her face and touched her arms, brushing his fingers lightly over her breasts. He kissed her nipples through her bra and began the challenge of removing it. Once her breasts were revealed to him he cupped them both and tasted them.

"You are so beautiful," he said again, so quietly, so reverently that she almost missed it.

Lynda reached for him and reveled in the feel of his naked flesh. Together they removed the last of their clothing. Michael protected them both. He entered her gently. They fit together perfectly, moving together as though their bodies had always known each other. Michael and Lynda stared into each other's eyes as they made love. She wanted to look away but couldn't. She wanted to hold some part of herself back but the intensity of Michael's lovemaking drew her like a moth to a flame. Their bodies glistened with a sheen of sweat. Michael drove into her harder and harder. Lynda bit his shoulders and dug her nails into his back in response. She growled when he began to slow down. Lynda grabbed his hips and pulled them to her with a ferocity that made him chuckle, "If that's the way you want it woman."

She was driven further and further into herself. Lynda exploded and cried out, her spasms, almost pushing Michael right outside of her, then he dove into her one final time and he joined her in ecstasy, shaking with the force of his release.

"Oh, Lynda, Lynda," he said, exhausted and awed.

Lynda loved the feel of this big man on top of her. She felt safe and cherished. She nuzzled his shoulder and he rolled over, pulling her with him, still too spent to really speak.

She sighed contentedly. "Well, I hope that was good for you too," she muttered to herself.

Michael just laughed and hugged her tight. Sleep came easily to him. Lynda studied him, so peaceful, so naked in her bed. Her mind was racing, her heart was lost—or was it found?

Chapter 10

The next morning Lynda stretched lazily in her bed, relishing in the sweet achiness of her body. Michael rolled over and snuggled into her, tickling her arm with his stubble. She ran her fingers through his mussed-up dark hair and his eyes opened to look at her. They flashed with the memory of last night and settled to a look of guarded hope.

"How are you feeling this morning?" he asked.

Lynda felt like a whole new world had opened before her. Her body hummed with wanton desire. She was free. Free to live and love without David. Free to live and love for herself. Free to have Michael for herself. There seemed only one way to truly answer his question. She rolled on top of him, happy for the mystery of morning wood, and showed this marvelous man just how she felt. She hadn't yet thought of her son.

Afterward, as they lay satisfied and breathing hard in each other's arms, Michael said, 'So I guess that means you have no second thoughts about last night."

Sighing contentedly, she said, "I guess so. How about you, doctor? Any second thoughts about me?"

"Honestly, Lynda, my only thought is, what did I do to deserve this? I am half afraid you are going to come to your senses and leave me in the dust."

"I'm not going anywhere. I'm just happy that my being a mom doesn't scare you off. You know I have to put Sean first, and yet you are still here." Sean, she thought, I wonder how messy this is going to get with him?

"I'll be here as long as you'll have me."

"Be careful what you wish for there, Dr. Cameron. You could be here for a very long time." Sometimes my brazenness surprises me. "You could save me a lot of money on batteries."

Michael laughed at that and lightly slapped her on her cute little ass. "You go get showered pretty lady and I'll make you breakfast."

As Michael headed downstairs to make Lynda the promised breakfast, she hopped in the shower. As the hot water poured over her, Lynda wondered at herself. She stretched and flexed under the hot stream and smiled at the happy achiness of her body. Why wasn't she more stressed about all of this? Why wasn't she more worried about Sean's reaction to this? Why wasn't she more worried about what to say when she got downstairs? She laughed at herself as she worried about why she wasn't more worried. I guess great sex is good stress relief, she told herself, just enjoy the moment, the real world and it's problems will come at me soon enough. Thus she entered the kitchen with a smile on her face and peace in her heart. The kitchen looked as though every bowl and pot in her house had been used, but the room smelled of homemade pancakes, hot maple syrup, and chicken/apple sausage.

"Mmm, smells good."

"I hope you like it," Michael said. "Breakfast is about the only thing I can cook."

"Fine by me. I hardly ever have the energy to cook in the morning."

He served them each a plate of pancakes and sausage and blessedly hot and strong coffee. She tried not to glance at the dishes as she dug in. He caught her though, and followed her gaze. "Don't worry, I'll clean up too!"

Guiltily, she caught his eye. "I'll help." She looked at the clock. "Oh my gosh, is that the time?" It was already 8:30 a.m. "You're going to be late, Michael, you have to get out of here."

"Relax, I already called Susan and told her I was running late."

Rolling her eyes she said, "I'll bet she was thrilled."

"No, but I do own the practice and fifteen minutes isn't that much to ask once in a while."

"Fifteen minutes? You're not going home to change and shave?"

"No, I have a razor at the office that'll do."

"Well, don't worry about the dishes. I'll take care of them."

He looked back at the pile and said, "It's kind of a lot. Why don't you leave them and I'll do them tonight."

"Okay," Lynda agreed. She paused. "Nice way to finagle an invitation over for dinner tonight."

"I thought so," he said smugly. He kissed Lynda quickly on the lips and headed off to work.

The ten-minute drive wasn't exactly enough time for him to process what he had just done. He had never felt so comfortable so quickly with a woman. She was not the kind of woman to have a fling and he had just invited himself over for dinner, and yet seeing her again so quickly somehow felt right. She felt like a home he'd never really known and he wanted to get as much of it as he could. And my God, the sex was amazing. Work, however, was not exactly what he had hoped for. While no more graffiti decorated his clinic, and the protestors had not yet arrived for the day, there was yet another police car parked outside. Inside Detective Hughes, who'd been monitoring the situation with the protestors, was busy talking to Susan and the waiting room was half full of people being conspicuously quiet.

It wasn't until lunchtime that he had a chance to ask Susan about the police.

Susan was not her usual calm self. All morning she'd been fussing with files and distracted with patients. She had unconcealed bags under her eyes, as if she hadn't slept.

When she finally got Michael alone in his office at lunch, she positively gushed nervous energy.

"Susan, what's wrong?"

"Oh Michael," she all but cried as she rushed to his arms.

He hugged her back, perplexed. She was usually the most in control, undemonstrative person he'd ever met.

"I don't understand it, Michael," she said. She finally released him. "I've been getting awful calls at home, at my new number."

He looked at her, concerned. "But isn't your number unlisted? You've always been so careful."

"That's just it. It is unlisted and it's brand new, just since the move. I've barely given it out to anyone. I mean, at first it was just hang-ups and I thought it was nothing more than those annoying automated telemarketing machines, but last night it changed. I got two heavy breathers close together, then a call with vile threats. He was disgusting and graphic. I hung up on him and unplugged my phone."

"Oh Susan, I'm so sorry. You could have called me."

"I did," she said flatly. "You weren't home."

"You could have tried my cell. And this morning when I called, you could have told me then. I would have come right away!"

Susan bit her lip. Her eyes were glossy with unshed tears. "I … I didn't know. I thought that you wouldn't want to be interrupted. I mean this Lynda seems to be important to you."

"Oh Susan," Michael said. "We are friends, aren't we, despite everything?" He hugged her again.

With her head burrowed in his chest, he missed her smile entirely.

Around four that afternoon he called Lynda to explain the situation to her and to tell her that he'd be late because after work he was going with Susan back to her place, just to reassure her that it was safe.

"Are you sure you're still coming?"

"Yes, I'm still coming," he said, noting the skeptical tone in her voice, "but I have to help Susan. She was really scared by the phone calls."

Relenting, Lynda said, "Well, I can understand that. Sometimes being a single woman is really hard." Lynda's mind was racing between suspicion and strategy. She didn't doubt that the calls had been scary but she would bet anything Susan could play it for all it was worth. And Michael might or might not see it coming. At this point, though, she decided, she shouldn't play the suspicious, jealous, lover. She should be generous. "Please give her my sympathy. If there is anything I can do, let me know."

Michael sighed audibly. "Thanks for understanding. I'll be over as soon as I can."

"If something comes up and you can't make it, will you please let me know?" She couldn't completely hide the worry in her voice.

"Hey, you know that I want to be with you. You and Sean. You know you have nothing to worry about, nothing to be jealous about, don't you?"

"I'm trying," Lynda said honestly.

Michael chuckled in spite of himself. "You're jealous," he taunted.

"Maybe a little, but don't go getting all big headed about it or anything."

He laughed out loud. The truth was, it did feel damn good. He hung up, leaving his very confident, very male laughter ringing in Lynda's ears.

Sean and Karen had been working at the kitchen table on their homework after school and had overheard his mother's end of the conversation. Sean merely raised his eyebrow questioningly. Lynda filled him in on the details.

"And?" Sean asked.

"And …" Lynda hesitated.

"And your mom thinks Susan is going to make a play for Michael," Karen answered.

Sean looked from Karen to his mom, open-mouthed. "No way!" he said.

Lynda nodded. "Yup. I just don't think he'll see it coming. And I don't know how smooth she'll be, but I bet she's good."

"Oh you guys, women are so suspicious!"

Karen and Lynda gave each other a knowing look.

Sean waved his hands in disgust.

"Besides," Sean said, as he turned to leave this tawdry conversation behind, "Michael's a smart guy, he knows if he steps out on you, Mom, he'll have to answer to me."

Karen turned to follow Sean, and then looked back to Lynda. "Don't worry, my money's on Michael high-tailing it out of there once he figures her out."

"I hope you're right, or better yet, I hope I'm wrong about Susan."

Susan's apartment was cozy and efficient. It was immaculately neat, photo ready, in fact. The walls were a shade of lavender that was just barely not white. Michael felt very large in this small space. He casually looked for any evidence of their old life together and was surprised to find their wedding picture framed on the phone table. He recognized the only original painting on the wall, a Denise Natanson they'd purchased together. It had been his favorite, and he never thought she'd really liked it. He thought she'd taken it in the divorce just to hurt him or more likely because it had appreciated in value.

"I see you still have Denise's painting. I always thought you'd sell it."

Susan touched his arm. "I just couldn't. I always remember going to the artist open studios with you and how much we loved meeting her and how happy you always were when you looked at it. I didn't want to let go of that."

Michael tried hard to hide his surprise and puzzlement.

"Surprised? Bet you thought I didn't have a sentimental bone in my body."

Michael shrugged a little sheepishly. "I think there's probably a lot we never really knew about each other." The failure of his marriage still loomed in his psyche.

Susan just smiled. Looking around her apartment she said, "I know it isn't much, but …"

"It's fine. I can't imagine you're here all that much anyway, so why pay for space you don't use?" In truth, he was surprised. The Susan he knew was used to demanding the finest things in life. The furniture that was here was good quality but hardly what she'd insisted on when she'd decorated their place. Susan turned back to the front door. She set the deadbolt and put her purse down on the entryway table.

Still looking around the apartment Michael said, "I'm sorry things didn't work out for you with your finance guy." He was actually sincere and happy with himself that he was.

Susan still had her back to Michael when he spoke. Her face contorted angrily for a moment, then flashed to scared, then settled on sad. "Oh well," she said, "he wasn't you." She turned and looked at him intently, but he looked away.

"Well," he said, "everything looks fine here. So I'll head out now."

She grabbed his arm. "Oh, Michael, don't go," she begged. "What if he calls again?"

She looked so small, so scared. "Susan, it'll be okay. Just do what Detective Hughes said. Why don't you put his card by the phone? And if you just can't face having to deal with it," she still clung to him, "we can take the phone off the hook."

Batting her eyelashes slightly she looked up at him. "But I feel so alone. Can't you stay just a little longer?" Her breasts grazed his arm ever so subtly.

Flustered and a little confused, Michael backed up, bumping into the alley kitchen's half wall. "Maybe just a little more, then I really have to go."

Susan's shoulders dropped in relief. "Thank you. I just don't want to be alone right now." She backed away and said, "Why don't you help yourself to some wine? I'm just going to go get out of my work clothes."

Michael felt in need of a glass of wine, so he went to the kitchen and found a bottle he well recognized. It was from his uncle's small vineyard in Sonoma, California. Tears welled up in Michael's eyes. His uncle was the closest thing he'd had to a real father, and he'd only been gone six months. He poured himself a glass full of memories. The small vineyard had always been his oasis. It was where he went to lick his wounds. After his parents had died so many years ago, after Susan had left him. His uncle didn't talk much but he understood more about life than just about anyone he knew, and he gave Michael the space he needed to figure things out for himself.

Michael smiled, remembering what his uncle had said when he showed up hurt and angry the day Susan had moved out. "Son," he said, in that slow, wise way farmers do, "Are you sure you're missing her or rather is it what she should have been to you?" Michael had railed against the idea at the time, but eventually came to realize the truth in what the old man had said.

"My Caroline loved me as I was, she did, brought out the best in me too—well, most of the time, anyways." His uncle's eyes had teared up and he had wiped them away unashamed. "She was the best of me, that woman was, truly the best of me." Michael still kicked himself for not getting to know her as anything more than the happy, patient woman who baked, mended wounds, and made things work. He'd been in medical school when she died.

Susan emerged from the bedroom in a floor-length satin robe covering a lacy negligee. She couldn't help but see the nostalgia in Michael's face, and she smiled.

"You look good standing in my kitchen."

Michael looked at her, stunning and sleek in black satin. He looked at his glass of wine, not needing to guess at what his uncle would have him do. He put his glass down, walked over to Susan searching for the right words. She reached up to him and he caught her hands gently and stepped back.

"You seem more at ease now, so I'm going to leave. Don't hesitate to call Detective Hughes if you get scared." He turned on his heels and fled. He wasn't sure he fully understood what had just happened or why, but he knew he'd just made his uncle smile up in heaven.

Michael raced home, grabbed a few things and headed over to Lynda's.

Lynda couldn't help but look at the clock when she heard Michael's car in the driveway: 7:28. She caught Karen's eye, glanced at the clock, and smiled. Karen smiled back. A moment later the doorbell rang. Sean looked up from his dinner and said, "Sounds like Michael's here."

Lynda asked Sean to set another place at the table while she went to answer the door.

Michael presented Lynda with a very special bottle of wine. Over dinner he told Lynda, Sean, and Karen the story of the wine, a reserve syrah from his uncle's vineyard from a batch that was never sold. He told them about his aunt and uncle and the vineyard that had sadly became his six months ago.

"How often do you get up there?" Lynda asked.

Michael frowned. "Only about once a month. The place doesn't need me to run it, thank goodness. Serge, the vineyard guru, as I call him, manages it beautifully. My uncle had been doing less and less the last several years as he gradually retired."

"Do you make much money in the wine business?" Sean asked tactlessly.

Lynda shot him a frustrated look.

Michael just grinned. "Well, some people do, some don't but we usually break even at least."

"I bet it's beautiful up there," Karen said.

"It is," Michael said. "You guys should all come up some weekend."

Everybody's eyes widened.

"What?"

"Aaah, you just invited my teenage son and his girlfriend away for the weekend."

"Oh … I just thought, I mean Karen seems part of the gang. I assumed they'd have separate bedrooms."

Karen blushed at the conversation. She looked down and fussed with her napkin.

Lynda sighed. "I just don't want to be responsible for causing Karen any problems at home or at school."

Karen looked up quickly. "Mrs. B.?"

"High school is a cruel place, and going away for the weekend with a boy could make life difficult for you." Lynda bit her lip. Karen was such a great girl. More and more she was dressing as she was today: jeans that fit but not too tight, and a blouse instead of a tight t-shirt or crop top. She was wearing relatively subtle make-up. Lynda'd hate to see Karen slide backwards.

"Mrs. B.," Karen said, "I've never been what people thought I was." She avoided the s word. "They can say or think whatever they want. I have plans, I know what I want to be, and they won't stop me."

Michael felt totally in the dark listening to this conversation. He looked to Sean for illumination.

"People used to think that Karen was ..." he paused, "well, indiscriminate," he said in a moment of tactfulness.

"Really?"

"Yes," Karen said.

"Hmm, all I can say is, thank goodness high school ends and you never have to see any of those people ever again. College is the best," Michael said.

"C'mon, Mom, let her come," Sean pleaded.

"Your folks won't mind?" she asked Karen.

Karen's parents didn't seem to notice that their daughter had dinner at her house almost every night lately. They seemed pretty uninvolved, and it broke Lynda's heart. Sometimes teenagers needed just as much parenting as toddlers!

"Mrs. B.," Karen said, "I'm sure they won't mind. I mean, you are going to be there, after all, and ... well I'm sure that'll be enough for them."

Something in Karen's tone made Lynda pause. While Lynda thought she was telling the truth, she was equally sure there was something she wasn't saying. Lynda's heart reached out to this young woman. Her maternal instincts raged. Part of her wanted to take Karen in and adopt her, but that would be very awkward for Sean.

Michael watched the love and concern play on Lynda's beautiful face.

"So, it's settled then. How about we head up next weekend?" Michael said finally.

"Okay," said Lynda more than a little reluctantly.

"Thanks Mom," Sean said. "We've been working really hard, you know. Writing essays for college and doing up our applications and school and stuff. We're due for an adventure." He was grinning happily, clearly a little surprised at his good fortune.

Chapter 11

The next morning before Sean headed off to school Lynda forced herself to talk to him about his feelings about Michael. Sean had been pretty cool but that wasn't always a true measure of what was going on inside of him. She also wanted to make sure that he understood that she expected him and Karen to sleep in separate bedrooms. When Sean came down to the kitchen he was assaulted by the smell of pancakes and bacon. His delight and surprise at a midweek hot breakfast quickly gave way to suspicion. After filling his plate, sitting down and stuffing his mouth he said, "What's up?"

Lynda dusted her hands off on her apron and said, "Don't talk with your mouth full."

Sean grunted in response.

'Umm, well I wanted to check with you about your feelings about Michael and me and … "

Sean groaned and rolled his eyes. After swallowing he said, "Mom, it's early, do I really have to talk to you about my feelings?" His tone was tinged with amusement as he watched his mother, in perpetual motion, cleaning the dishes from preparing breakfast.

She caught his tone, relaxed a little, and looked at him, "Well yes, you do and we have to talk about the sleeping arrangements for you and Karen this weekend as well."

"So," he took another fork full of food and stuffed it in his mouth. "You get to have sex but I don't."

"Stop talking with your mouth full. And yes that is one way to sum it up."

He swallowed, "Kind of seems like a double standard, doesn't it?"

"Of course, but on the other hand I am an adult and you aren't quite there yet, besides," She bit her lip.

Sean watched her. She was thinking and he wasn't sure what was about to come out of her mouth next.

"You know, you really should take your time with Karen, physically I mean, make sure you don't push her. Sometimes a young man or an older one, too, can push without meaning too and I really don't want that for her. I don't want her to say 'yes' to something just so that she doesn't hurt your feelings, you know what I mean."

"Mom, relax, okay. This is me. You have been talking to me about women and sex and respect practically my whole life in one way or another. I know to let her call the shots. But hey, thanks for being worried about her. I mean, after all I am your son, your one and only child, your blood relation and all. Thanks for being worried about me and what's going on with me in the relationship."

Lynda looked at him truly horrified, "Oh baby, I'm so sorry. How are you? Is everything okay? Is she being good too you?" The questions spluttered out quickly and all jammed together, her concern was genuine and consuming.

Sean laughed as he forked another piece of pancake, "Gotcha."

Lynda laughed as she threw her dishtowel at him. It him square in the face and almost fell to his plate before he caught it. "Hey, I'm eating here," he said while still chewing.

"Stop talking with your mouth full!"

Later that afternoon when Lynda returned home from grocery shopping, she found Sean and Karen and Paul and Maddie all hanging out at her house. Happily, it took no more than a raised eyebrow for her to prompt Sean to help bring in the groceries. Paul and the girls automatically followed suit. The happy noise of the four of them told Lynda that things seemed to be very comfortable between the teenagers. The boys were loud and rough with each other, but the teasing all seemed comfortable. The girls were amused by the boys as girls usually are.

As Lynda was preparing dinner with the girls, she asked her son who was playing video games with Paul in the TV room, if his friends were all staying. Paul overheard this and said, "If you're cooking, we're staying. You can bet on that, Mrs. B."

Lynda laughed. "Okay then. Michael will be here too, just so you know." Back in the kitchen with the girls, a light bulb went on in Lynda's brain. She sent Maddie a questioning look. Karen caught this but didn't seem to know what to make of it.

Maddie looked at Lynda and didn't understand. "What is it Mrs. B?"

"Has Sean mentioned to you that I am dating Dr. Michael Cameron?"

Maddie put two and two together and Karen wasn't sure but she thought she just had too. Maddie turned to Karen but said nothing.

Karen wanted to put Maddie at ease. "I've met him, he's nice. He helped Sean and me out with our marketing paper." Karen's voice was deliberately light but her eyes were warm and she tried to send Maddie an unspoken communication of acceptance and sisterhood. Lynda's eyes went from one to the other. Maddie was tense; she looked at Lynda then back to Karen.

"Yeah, he's a nice man. He helped me deal with a problem I had a while back. I bet you can guess what it was."

Karen smiled at her, "It is nobody's business what it was, Maddie. Besides in my experience people think what they want to anyway, and life is rarely as black and white as people want it to be."

Maddie grimaced as she smiled, "Kind of ironic really, me being the good girl in everyone's eyes and you, well, you being the not-so-good girl shall we say."

Karen nodded and smiled, "Life's like that sometimes."

Maddie looked at her, "Life's a bitch,"

"Then you die," finished Karen.

Lynda laughed, "I had no idea people still said that."

"Retro is totally in, Mrs. B. Didn't you know that?" Maddie said.

"There's a lot I don't know, believe me." Lynda smiled at the girls. "Well, shall we get this dinner put together?" The three women talked and laughed as they made supper. When Michael arrived, he was surprised to see Paul and Maddie. But the only one who noticed the slight change in him was Lynda.

Maddie greeted him casually with a "Hi Dr. Cameron," and he countered with, "Please call me Michael." From then on out things were as loud, as fun, and as relaxed as they always were with a room full of hungry teenagers devouring a home-cooked meal.

A few days later, the convoy drive up to Sonoma was uneventful. It started appropriately enough with both men opening the car doors for their ladies—very elegant indeed. The moment was not spoiled by Sean's driver-side door sticking, once again, and needing some brute force to open and shut it. Sean and Karen drove in Sean's car while Lynda and Michael drove up in his Jag, each pair relieved to be listening to their own music.

The driveway up to the main house at the vineyard was lined on both sides by symmetrical fields of vines that had been recently harvested. The homestead was a warm, old farmhouse. This was no pretentious estate; it was a home that welcomed one and all. It was two stories with wood shingles on the roof. It had a big wrap-around porch littered with inviting rocking chairs, loveseats, and end tables.

As Lynda stepped out of the car, a breeze swirled around her, gently enveloping her in the fresh scents and smells of the country air.

The garage, if you could call it that, was kitty-corner to the left of the house as you faced the front. It was a two-story, four-car garage but double deep so it had room for eight. Lynda commented on the structure and Michael told her that that was Serge's domain. He lived upstairs and ran the shop on the main floor. The path going between the homestead and the shop led to the heart of the winemaking operation.

"We should ask Serge to give you guys the grand tour. He's the expert."

As though he had heard his name, Serge appeared, walking up the path. He was short and thick. His skin was weather worn and wrinkled. His fingernails looked as though they lived in soil. He had a crown of closely cropped white hair in a ring around a bald head. On his feet was a pair of greasy and well-worn workman's boots. His eyes were green and sharp. They carefully took in Lynda, then the two teenagers, as he approached Michael.

Focusing on his boss he said, "You made good time."

"That we did. Serge. Let me introduce you to our guests." Which he proceeded to do, rather formally.

Serge shook hands with them all in turn.

Lynda smiled at this man who reminded her of her grandfather: sharp as a tack, could learn just about anything, and who enjoyed being underestimated.

"Serge," she said, "would you consider giving us the grand tour at some point this weekend? There is nothing like learning from a master."

His eyes smiled in response to Lynda's flattery. "Of course, ma'am. It'd be my pleasure."

"Oh, thank you, and please—it's Lynda."

By this time Sean was poking around the shop.

"Oh man, Mom, Karen, you guys gotta see this. They have their own lathe and milling machine."

Lynda turned to Michael and Serge. "He's his father's son, insatiably curious about everything remotely technical."

Lynda and Karen headed over to the shop; Michael and Serge followed a few steps behind.

"She's a looker," Serge said quietly to his boss.

"She's more."

"Mmm. Good thing, that," Serge murmured as they caught up to the starry-eyed Sean.

Sean began peppering Serge with questions about what kinds of equipment and processes they used in making and bottling wine. Before long, they'd left the shop for the other out buildings and were all on a fascinating tour of a wine cave. Sean had questions about the chemistry of fermentation and how to measure and manage the process. They talked about the role of temperature and humidity control and the generators and back-up systems for environmental control of the cave and more.

Michael whispered to Lynda, "I don't think I've ever seen Serge have so much fun."

"Sean's having a blast too."

"I can tell."

Sean and Serge forged ahead, kindred spirits, deep in conversation, lost to the others. Karen eventually stopped trying to keep up with Sean and fell back with Michael and Lynda.

"Wow, those two may never stop," she said. "Is Sean always like this?"

"When he's around something new and technical, yes, he is."

Karen thought for a moment and watched him closely. He was so animated and intense. He was completely happy. "I hope he never loses it."

Lynda looked at Karen, and thought, "Wise woman."

"Don't worry, his father never did. He was like a kid in a candy store whenever he met experts at anything, who were willing to share what they knew and how they did what they did."

Michael shifted a little uncomfortably. That was the second time Lynda had mentioned her late husband, and he didn't know what to make of it. He stood stiffly, lost in his thoughts. Lynda elbowed him playfully.

"What's the matter? Jealous?"

Looking a little sheepish, he said, "What if I am, a little? It's hard to compete with a dead man." As soon as the words were out of his mouth he wanted to take them back. The shock on his face was a testament to his horror at himself. Of course she loved her husband and missed him and wished he wasn't dead. Seeing him in Sean was all she had left of him besides her memories.

Lynda's mind raced, scrambling for a way out of this moment.

Finally Karen said, "Well, I get what you mean, Michael. I mean, it is easy to idolize someone once they're gone and downplay their flaws and all, but I wouldn't worry if I were you, because Lynda knows he's gone and she's not and she seems to want to be with you,"

Michael and Lynda turned to Karen, he in relief and she in focused study. That was the second time today Karen had revealed her depth. Any concerns Lynda may have had about Sean's growing relationship with her vanished, then a whole new set rushed in—the too-much-too-soon, too-serious-too-intense kind. Oh well, she thought to herself, he's seventeen and besides who am I to talk? It's out of my hands now, if it was ever in them, she told herself.

That night at dinner the phone rang. They were all having dinner around a big oak table that could seat twelve comfortably. The country kitchen was spacious and light with big windows over the kitchen sink and French doors that opened out to the backyard. The chandelier over the table had been made by Michael's uncle many years before. The phone call was the first of many hang-ups. Ten minutes later when the phone rang again, Michael decided to let the machine get it. By the end of dessert everyone was on edge. No fewer than six crank calls had interrupted their dining.

Michael was frustrated and concerned, more about Lynda's reaction than about the calls themselves.

"That's it. I'm unplugging the phone," Michael said in disgust.

"What's going on, boss?" Serge asked. He had joined them for dinner. "You start giving out this number all of a sudden?"

"No."

Lynda looked at Michael. "You mean this number's unlisted?"

Michael nodded. This was the last thing he needed. He'd never ever had trouble from the clinic follow him here. Looking at Lynda, he saw that she was tense.

Karen and Sean were clearly not oblivious to the stress in the room.

"Mom, relax, it's only a few crank calls. What's the big deal? Don't let it ruin our fun."

She took a good look at her son, unsure how much to say, how much to worry. She held her breath in indecision.

Watching her, Michael felt like he could read her mind. He could feel her worry about worrying Sean, and her worry that she could be entering a world too dangerous for her and her son.

Michael sighed in resignation. "The big deal is," he said, as all eyes turned to his, "that there has been some trouble at the clinic lately—protesters and graffiti—and Susan, my office manager (Lynda noted that he didn't say ex-wife), got crank calls at her new unlisted home number a few days ago, and this could be related, though I don't see how, because this isn't my main home and practically no one has this number."

"I forgot about Susan," Sean said, "but this is probably just chaos theory at work."

Lynda seemed to relax a tiny bit. "So you really think it's just kids?" she said to Michael.

Serge slapped his forehead and said, "Man, I'm slow. Let's *69 'em and tell the parents what's going on."

Unfortunately, *69 didn't work. Then Sean declared that they should be heavy breathers when they answered the next call. Karen suggested they should all scream as loudly and shrilly as possible to hurt the kids' ears. And from there the discussion disintegrated into ridiculous counter-crank-call strategies, leaving everyone laughing and eager for the next call that never came.

After dinner Serge excused himself and retreated to his domain. Michael, with Lynda by his side, showed Sean and Karen to their separate rooms. Lynda's face was an open book of silent concern. "Relax," said Michael, "The floor creaks. You'll hear Sean if tries to head to Karen's room."

Lynda smiled at her man. He always knew just what to say.

Sean rolled his eyes in mock disgust at the two of them, "As long as your bed doesn't creak to loudly." He quipped back at the grown ups.

"Sean!" Lynda was horrified and blushing furiously.

Michael's jaw hung open momentarily at a loss for words, but Karen burst out laughing, which broke the tension.

Lynda glared at her son lovingly, "Goodnight."

"'Night Mom," he said sweetly as they went their separate ways.

As Lynda and Michael were getting ready for bed, she knew she had to confront the crank call issue head on.

"Those phone calls really scared me."

"I know, I'm sorry, but it is part of the territory."

She bit her lip. "Just how much harassment is normal and, more importantly, does it ever go beyond that?"

Michael sat beside her on the bed. "I don't practice in the Deep South or anything. I always have an unlisted number, and I've only had to change it once in the last five years. The graffiti on the clinic and the protesters harassing patients comes and goes, usually depending on what legislation is pending, but I've never experienced anything worse than this." He took her hand in his. "This is California. I mean, I own a flak jacket, but I've never worn it."

Lynda rested her head on his shoulder. She sighed. "It's just all so awful. I'm so grateful you do what you do for women, and that you do it here in California where it's relatively safe."

"But."

"But if it became unsafe, would you quit? I don't think so. You care too much about your patients to abandon them. And that's the way it should be. I just worry about bringing Sean into this. I'm his only parent. I have to be careful."

Michael held her there sitting on the bed, not knowing what to say. He didn't think there was any real danger, but he couldn't deny the horrors that pro-life terrorists had committed in other parts of the country, even in recent years. He wanted to sugarcoat things, but he couldn't bring himself to be anything other than straight with her. He had to be honorable. She deserved that much, and that's who he had to be when he was with her.

Finally he said, "I can't tell you what to do, Lynda. I wish I could tell you that I know for certain I'll be safe, and that you and Sean will be too. But no one can say that for certain, not really."

"I know. And I'm not about to let a couple of preteen pranksters scare me away. This just takes some getting used to, that's all." Her mind made up, for the moment at least, she started to relax. She wanted to enjoy the fresh country air blowing in the window. She wanted to enjoy this space, Michael's haven from the world. The room was so male and yet so gentle. The furniture was big and solid but with rounded edges. The bed was only a queen size but it had a hand made quilt on it that was soft and worn and full of the colors of fall. Lynda wanted to enjoy him. She wanted to live in the moment. She wanted to love him and love life again. She wanted to be free.

In the quiet, Michael could hear her breathing slow and feel her body relax. He held her closer. He was suddenly stunned when he realized how scared he'd been that she wouldn't relax, wouldn't stay with him. He'd only known this woman a short time and already she meant more to him than anyone ever had. He couldn't imagine being without her. He clung to her in the relief that he wouldn't have to.

"I'm not letting you go, Lynda. I'll do everything in my power to keep you and Sean safe from my world. You have to know that."

She looked into those earnest brown eyes, caressed his cheek, and said, "I know, we can handle a few phone calls just fine."

She kissed him gently at first but he responded with a hunger and intensity that made her quiver. His need was overpowering. He attacked her clothes, groaning in frustration at the snug jeans he had once admired. He finally flung them aside, and with Lynda's help made quick work of his own clothes. Barely pausing for breath, he dove into her. She was ready for him, his passion awaking her own. His need thrilled her as her body moved with his. He couldn't get enough of her, couldn't get deep enough. He plunged into her again and again, faster and faster, reaching for her soul. He collapsed on top of her moments later, spent and dazed.

He felt her shaking under him as the blood returned to his brain.

"Oh Lynda, oh my God, I'm so sorry," he said, rolling off her. It took him a few seconds to register that she was laughing.

"You're laughing? I thought … I mean, …" He was confused.

Lynda reached up and touched his face. "Dr. Michael Cameron, you are definitely good for my ego."

He just stared at her.

"I didn't give you any time to …"

She just laughed some more. "No, but I'm sure you'll make up for it before long."

He nodded at the amused woman beside him. "I will, I promise." He was bewildered.

Lynda stretched like a cat and got up to get a glass of water. She was totally unself-conscious. She was totally confident and completely happy.

Michael watched her. "I'm beginning to realize that I don't know very much about women at all. I thought you'd be, I don't know, less than pleased."

"Oh, Michael, love," she turned to him, "I have never felt so desired. True, you rushed, but I could've said no if I wanted to, and you'll take care of me yet. I have faith in you."

She did have faith in him, and he felt it. She trusted him and he suddenly realized that he'd forgotten what that felt like, if he'd ever really known at all.

When she returned to bed, Michael couldn't take his eyes off of her. "I love you," he said. His voice was strong and tender, and his eyes shone with the truth of his words.

"I love you," Lynda said not in response, an "I love you too," but a simple statement of truth, and that was how he heard it.

He caressed her cheek and kissed her gently, feather light. He kissed her eyelids, her temples, her cheekbones. He began to make love to her. He took his time and loved each and every part of her, thanking God for this woman in his life. He kissed and caressed every inch of her beautiful skin, memorizing its texture and taste. He gave her the most intimate of kisses, sucking and teasing her with his mouth and just when she thought she couldn't take anymore he slid his fingers inside her wet heat and simultaneously stimulated her beyond anything she had ever known. She quivered and shook and bit her lip trying not to cry out as the heat built and swirled inside her. Then he entered her. He moved to excite her. Lynda couldn't hold back anymore. She clawed at him and growled in need. She cried out as pleasure exploded throughout her as she spasmed again and again and again. She came so hard Michael was barely able to stay inside her but he was beyond thinking. He drove and pounded himself into her, unwilling to leave her. Tears fell down her face as Michael exploded inside her. They clung to each other as tears kissed their cheeks, at a loss for words to express the depth and intensity of what they'd just shared. And that was how they fell asleep, clinging to each other, spent and blanketed in God's love and peace.

Chapter 12

The morning dawned sunny and clear. It was the perfect day to explore. Lynda wanted to visit the nearest town to Michael's vineyard and so off they went with Sean and Karen in tow. The town was typical of the area, cute and quaint with several art galleries and other concessions to the local tourist trade. It had one main street with a grocery store at one end, a used bookstore at the other, restaurants in the middle and art galleries and boutiques scattered throughout. In the window of one boutique was a beautiful dress that caught Karen's eye. It was a simple cotton dress, a cranberry print with little flowers in white and pink. It had a mid-calf length skirt that flared out ever so slightly at the hem. The delicately scooped neckline gave it a classic and very feminine style.

Lynda saw Karen's gaze as she stared at the dress. "You should try it on, I bet it would look great on you."

Karen started to refuse but then Sean jumped in and then Michael too insisted that she should try it on, so all four went to the little boutique and Karen found a dress in her size and tried it on. It fit, as so few garments do, as though it had been made for her and her alone. When she stepped out of the dressing room she knew she looked good but she wasn't altogether comfortable, either. Sean gave a low whistle when he saw her. "Wow," he said.

"Wow is right, you look amazing Karen," Michael said.

Lynda smiled at Karen's embarrassed pleasure at the compliments. "They're right Karen, it was made for you."

Karen touched the cotton in her fingertips. It felt smooth and soft. She spun around and the skirt flared out around her legs. "It is a beautiful dress," she said when she stopped.

"We'll take it," said Sean. He turned to the clerk and asked then to ring it up.

Karen was taken aback. "But Sean, what are you doing? I can't afford this dress. I was just trying it on for fun."

"Babe," he said, "I can't afford for you not to have this dress. It's yours." He turned and gave the clerk his money.

"Why don't you wear it out of the store?" Lynda said. "We can put your other clothes in the bag. The black boots you were wearing with your jeans should go with the dress just fine."

That's exactly what she did. Karen kissed Sean as they were leaving the store. She had never walked taller or glowed quite so much as she did the rest of that afternoon. Her joy brought pleasure to them all.

Lynda must have dragged Michael into every little art gallery on the strip that day. He loved every moment of it; he loved the way Lynda's eyes shone in their excitement. He felt like he was seeing everything for the first time because he was seeing it with her. They laughed and argued playfully about the art, what they liked and disliked, about what art was and was not. They looked at crafts and homemade glass blown jewelry. They browsed in the used bookstore for almost an hour. When it was time to head back all four of them were tired and happy.

That night at dinner the crank calls began again, but this time Michael quickly unplugged the phone. He resented the cloud on an otherwise perfect day. Seeing Lynda with Sean, watching him, teasing him, and trusting him with Karen made his heart warm and ache at the same time. He had never longed for a child of his own as much as he did now. Susan and he had never made time for children. If he was being honest with himself, he had to admit that after being married to her a short while, he couldn't really picture her being a mom to his kids. So he just let it go. As he was so involved with his work, it was easy to put off what he didn't want to face. He probably wouldn't have made much of a dad at that point in his life anyway, he mused, but now … now it was too late. The most he could hope for was to be included in this family before him. He could still have kids, true, and Lynda might, but with a senior in high school he didn't think she'd want to start over. Still, maybe he should ask anyway. It's not like having kids was a deal breaker for him, but having Lynda definitely was.

Up in their room that night—funny how quickly it changed from his room to their room—he struggled to find the words to ask Lynda about kids.

Lynda watched Michael closely. He was a little distracted and tense. She wondered if the phone call had upset him; maybe he was worried about Susan.

"Michael, maybe you should call Susan and see if she is still getting crank calls too."

He stopped pacing and looked at her, perplexed. "Huh? Oh, that can wait. Do you think I should report these calls to the police?" This is not what he wanted to be talking about. "I'll report them in the morning. The truth is there's nothing they can do unless the calls keep coming and the caller is using an easy-to-find phone. Then they can be asked to stop calling."

Lynda wasn't sure what was going on with him; he still seemed uptight, and she'd tried hard to be really calm about the calls and understanding about his witch of an ex-wife, not that she was jealous or anything.

She sat on the bed and watched him fidget with the knickknacks on the shelf.

"Enough, Michael, whatever it is, spit it out!" Patience was not always her strong suit.

He exhaled audibly. "Okay, the thing is that I don't want you to freak out on me, because I'm expecting you to say no way in hell and that's really okay, but I thought I ought to put it out there since I was thinking about it." He paused to take a breath and Lynda's mind raced, trying to figure out what was coming.

"I was watching you with Sean today. He's an amazing kid, by the way, and, well, you're an incredible mom, truly. I assume you wouldn't consider becoming a mom again. No, of course not. Forget I mentioned it."

He looked so pained Lynda said, "Hey, Michael, sit down beside me here. I love you, but I'm in my forties. I had Sean early and I'm almost done. He's almost out of the house. Babies are hard, really hard, and I just can't imagine starting over now. I probably couldn't even if we wanted to. If I were ten years younger it'd be different, but I'm not."

He nodded, unsurprised.

"Are you sure that's okay with you? I mean, I do understand the need to have kids."

He held Lynda in his arms. "What I need is you. One miracle a lifetime is more than most men get."

"You're sure?" As the words came out of her mouth a startling thought came to her.

"I'm sure."

She tensed, thinking hard.

"What?" Michael asked.

She looked at him. "You swear you're not playing with me?"

Now Michael was worried. "I'm not, I promise."

"This all came to you today? Not before?"

"Y-e-s. It was watching you guys today that really made me wish I had that too. Why?"

She believed him. She wasn't sure why, but she did. "Well, then you have a powerful subconscious, mister, because ..."

"What are you talking about?"

"Last night."

"Last night was incredible, almost ..." he hesitated, "holy."

"And ..."

"And what?" Michael looked truly upset.

Lynda sighed. "It was beautiful and holy and what did we forget?"

Michael thought. He slapped his forehead. No wonder she thought he was playing games.

"Oh my God. I'm so sorry. Look, we'll run out and get you an E.C. right now." He grabbed her hand and stood up, tugging her with him.

"What's an E.C.?"

"Emergency contraception, it used to be called the morning-after pill. It's two pills, really, but it's very effective in preventing pregnancy. You'll probably be nauseous. Come on, I'll tell you on the way to the pharmacy. I'll write the scrip."

Lynda just stood there.

Michael turned to her. "Oh, Lynda, I'm so sorry. I just wasn't thinking. I swear it wasn't more than that." After all these years, Michael couldn't believe what he, of all people, had done. "I could just kick myself. I can't believe I didn't protect you."

Lynda looked at the very distressed doctor by her side. "It takes two, Michael."

"Yeah, but …"

"Yeah but, me too. Listen, I don't think we need to rush out to the pharmacy. In my most fertile years I had to try for months to get pregnant with Sean, and then in the years afterward nothing happened. So I don't think we need to worry on that front." Her eyes momentarily dimmed at the memory of all those months of disappointment. But Sean was more blessing than anyone deserved, teenager guy stuff and all. She looked up at Michael, relieved at his obvious distress and sincerity. "Never a dull moment, eh Michael?"

He sat on the bed, wrapped his arms around Lynda's waist, and rested his head against her shoulder. "And to think I usually come up here for peace."

Lynda laughed and hugged him back. "At least this will be an easy drama to avoid repeating."

"Definitely." Michael laughed as he reached for his bedside table drawer. Grinning mischievously, he said, "You know what they say, 'Practice makes perfect.'"

Later that night Karen was up late watching Letterman when Michael came downstairs to make himself some tea, Lynda was sound asleep but he was still restless. He poked his head in the TV room and saw Karen there, sad and alone.

"Hey there," he said.

She looked up, surprised. "Oh hi, Michael."

He walked into the room and sat, sort of perched on the edge of the sofa next to her. "Letterman, huh?"

"Yeah."

"Can't sleep?"

"Nah, but I don't need much."

Michael paused, sensing something was weighing on her. He put his elbows on his knees as he leaned forward. He slowly reached out and squeezed her knee reassuringly before sitting back keeping his upper body open and loosely clasping his hands in front of him.

"Your folks okay with you being here?"

"Here, here or being at Sean and Lynda's all the time you mean? Yeah, whatever, they don't care."

"You are safe here, you know."

She looked at him sideways and turned back to the TV. "I know."

Another pause followed.

"I'm here if you want to talk. Lynda too."

She nodded, not taking her eyes off the set. "It's a little weird right now with Sean."

Michael nodded. "I'm sure it is."

"He doesn't know … about me."

Michael's mind raced, were his suspicions correct? "I think he can handle it, Karen. He loves you." He was terrified of saying the wrong word, of closing the small opening that had begun.

"How'd you know?" She still stared at the TV. Her voice was a monotone.

"I didn't, not for sure"

"Oh."

Michael tentatively took her hand in his. "Karen now is a good time to start healing. You have people in your life who love you. There are lots of people to talk to who know what they are doing. Let me help you find the right person for you."

She looked at him. "Okay." She turned back to the TV. "I love Sean, you know, I really do. But how do I tell him what my father did to me?" She laughed sardonically. "He hasn't touched me in years, you know. He lost interest when I turned thirteen. So really it didn't last very long—only a couple of years. I guess his 'compulsion' is very specific. But Sean is so good, so pure."

"Maybe, but he is not ignorant of the world. Remember when Lynda made Paul baby-sit Sarah after she helped Maddie?"

"Yeah. She made Sean read some book about the myth of the slut or something."

"Wow, I didn't realize. That does sound like a very Lynda thing to do," Michael said.

"Yeah. Sean said something about it to me once. I didn't know what to think. I just figured he was trying to let me know that he didn't believe all the rumors about me. Maybe I should read it too. Who knows I could learn something and maybe it would give me a way to talk to Sean about things?" She paused. "Paul and Maddie are actually still together, you know."

"Really?"

"Yeah. They seem happy, too."

"Good for them."

"Maddie thinks Lynda is a saint; I think I agree with her."

Michael chuckled. "She is amazing. Just flawed enough to make her perfection tolerable."

Karen laughed. "She's so funny when she gets mad. Her eyes flash and you know she's going to blow."

"I know. Her nostrils flare and you know she's going to let fly."

"Yeah, but how is it she manages not to say anything cruel?"

"I asked her that once. She said it was years of excellent therapy."

"No way. Lynda in therapy? It's hard to picture."

"I know, but she said that's where she learned how to be who she wanted to be."

"No kidding? It kind of makes me feel normal, you know?"

"Yeah, I do," Michael said. "If it's good enough for Lynda, then it's good enough for the rest of us."

Karen spoke with a quiet, steady voice, "About finding me someone to talk to, I think I'm ready."

Michael nodded, relieved. This was big and he wanted some help with it. "I'll ask around and find someone great and if they don't fit well with you we'll just keep looking 'til we get the right person for you. Don't worry, I'm good at this." Interviewing therapists was something he had confidence in his ability to do well.

Karen nodded and half smiled at him, "Thanks." She was surprised at how much lighter she felt having finally told somebody. She had figured, quite correctly in fact, that Michael had heard much worse many times over in his practice. Despite being a man, he was a safe person to talk to.

The next day Michael dutifully reported the crank calls to the police and gave the investigator the name of the investigator handling Susan's case in Altos Verde in the South Bay. He didn't expect anything to come of it, but it couldn't hurt. The drive home was uneventful. Sean took Karen home and Michael took Lynda to his place. He wanted her to see it, but as they got closer he started to get nervous. He also hated keeping what Karen had confided to him from her but he had no choice, it just wasn't his place. He'd find somebody, the very best somebody for Karen to work with though and he'd do it right away.

Lynda teased him. "What, are you afraid you left your dirty laundry on the floor?"

He barely smiled.

"Aw, come on, I live with a teenager. It can't be that bad."

"I just haven't put all that much effort into the place recently," he admitted. Thinking about it he wondered what it would look like through her eyes. Would it be sterile and cold? What would she think it said about him?

Michael lived in a modern townhouse near downtown Mountain View. It was open concept with high ceilings. The furniture was leather and glass, elegantly styled but looking like a decorator had chosen it. Only the art softened the space. It was this that Lynda gravitated to when she entered the apartment. Michael had a Graham French print beautifully framed that was so warm and romantic. He had a couple of original paintings with brighter colors and evocative of happy daily life. Lynda looked around the room. The art was the only thing reflective of the Michael she had come to know.

"Hey, where are all your books?"

He led her to his home office. Lynda laughed out loud at her first sight of it. "It looks like a college professor's rabbit warren." Michael shrugged. The desk was disorganized and the walls were lined with mismatching bookcases crammed to overflowing with books. Many were medical books and journals, but there was also an eclectic selection of novels and biographies. The tour concluded in the master bedroom. It was dominated by an unmade king-sized bed and only mildly decorated with dirty clothes. Michael tried to kick them under his bed.

"I, ah, packed in a hurry for the weekend," he said, as he led her back to the living room. "Well, this is my place, such as it is."

Lynda sat on the designer sofa and looked up at him. "I see you have a lot left over from your days with Susan."

"I suppose."

"Tell me about the art, especially the Graham French. Tell me about what you love about this place."

Half an hour later, Michael was still telling stories of going to second-hand bookstores and artist open studios meeting artists and buying pieces that grabbed him. He was so animated. Lynda just loved the way his eyes lit up with excitement and humor, regaling her with stories of his life. It was a life he had almost forgotten about, it seemed to him as he talked about it, until now, until this weekend. The weekend that they had just shared, buying used books and looking at art, this was where their lives intersected. Their interests converged and melded together so easily. Seeing this, seeing him so happy gave Lynda a kind of comfort as she thought about the future that might one day be theirs. Finally she looked at the clock on her cell phone and reluctantly admitted that it was time for her to go.

"Can I stay over?" Michael asked hopefully, somewhat expectantly too.

Lynda hesitated. "I'd like that, but … I feel like I need some time to check in with Sean. He probably won't talk to me much, but I want to try to see where things are with him and Karen and how he's feeling about you and me."

"I'd be lying if I said I wasn't disappointed, but I understand." He was imagining a cold shower and a long, sleepless night in front of him.

Fifteen minutes later he dropped her off at her place, kissed her goodbye outside her door, and dutifully left her to be a good mom.

It was only after he got home that he gave himself a chance to worry about who the hell had been calling him up at the vineyard. He checked his answering machine, half expecting it to be full of hang-ups. If someone was targeting him because of the clinic, surely they would call here. Much to his relief there was only one message waiting for him.

It was from Susan. "Michael," she had said, "If you're there, pick up." She paused. "Oh yeah, I forgot, you're up at the vineyard this weekend. Oh well, I just wanted to let you know that the calls seem to have stopped here."

A thought flashed through his brain so quickly he missed it. But there was something odd in her voice. Actually, come to think of it, he was surprised she'd forgotten he was at the vineyard. When he told her last week at the office, she had icily responded with, "Moving kind of fast, aren't you?" Somehow he thought having Susan be even a little jealous ought to be more enjoyable. Oh well, she'll just have to get used to it.

Reluctantly he picked up the phone to return her call.

"Hello."

"Hi, Susan, it's Michael."

"I know your voice, Michael. Are you back in town?"

"Yes. I just got home and got your message. I'm glad the calls stopped. You must be relieved."

"Oh, I am ... so how was your weekend en famille?"

"Good." He wanted to discuss Lynda with Susan even less than he wanted to discuss Susan with Lynda.

"Do I hear a but?" she said, almost cheerfully.

"Would you believe I got crank calls up there?"

"No?"

"Yeah, but at least it didn't spoil the weekend." Why had he said that? I guess when you've spent a lot of time with someone habit can make it harder to censor yourself.

"Oh well, that's good," she said, sounding like she almost meant it. Michael knew her too well—almost. He had to get off the phone.

"Well, I'll see you tomorrow, okay?"

"Of course. I'll see you at the office."

As he hung up the phone he wondered for the thousandth time since his divorce, if working together was really such a good idea. But no one knew the office like Susan. He hated all the day-to-day administration, and she was so good at it. What was it Lynda had told him her best friend always said, "Just another pothole on the road to glory"? Yep, that summed it up about right.

Chapter 13

After carefully negotiating his Mom's inquisition about him and Karen, the last thing Sean felt like doing was discussing it all over again with Paul. And yet somehow he was on the phone with his best friend doing just that.

"So?" Paul said demandingly, "Come on give me details!"

Sean sighed, "No."

"Aw come on man, I'll bet she taught you a thing or two."

Sean felt like he was between a rock and a hard place. He cared about Karen, truly, but as much as he didn't want to hurt her reputation, such as it was, he didn't want to look like a pathetic virgin either.

"It's really nobody's business Paul, grow up would you." Sean was impatient and exasperated.

Paul chuckled, "So did you grow up at all this weekend?" His tone rattled Sean.

"If I did do you really think I'd tell you?" Sean knew he should just be honest and say that nothing happened but the words stuck in his throat.

"Okay, okay," Paul laughed. "Have it your way but remember, take it from me, play safe."

"Always," Sean said before he could stop himself.

Paul cackled, "I knew it! I bet she was awesome, knowing everything she does. You lucky dog!"

Sean held the phone in a death grip. He felt like a dog. He started to sweat. "Yeah well you can keep your ideas to yourself, my friend. I really don't want to be fresh meat to the gossip mongers at school, okay?"

"Yeah, sure, whatever."

"Promise," Sean insisted.

"Fine," Paul said, "Spoilsport."

Monday Lynda met her best friend Shelly for lunch. They had a lot to catch up on. They were eating at Chili's, one of their regular lunch places. The booths and the loud ambient noise gave them privacy and freedom to talk, to bitch and to gossip to their hearts content. They ususaly ordered the same things when they were there. Shelly got the Old Timer Burger, medium, no cheese and Lynda had the Philly Cheese steak.

"So how is Sean?" Shelly asked.

"Good. I didn't get a lot out of him about him and Karen. In a way I think his dating Karen is making the whole me-and-Michael thing easier for him."

"That's good. Just how often is Dr. Michael over anyway?"

"A lot."

"Mmm."

"Almost every night for dinner," Lynda said.

"Just dinner?"

Lynda just smiled. "It's just so easy being with him. He fits into the family so well."

"And you're sure you can deal with his job, because you know that's not going to change?"

"Yeah, I'm sure. I mean, as long as Sean and I are safe, which we are. I support him in what he does. You know that. It's not a job I want, but I'm glad there are doctors like him doing it."

Shelly nodded. "Me too. But judging by the news lately, anti-choice activity is on the rise across the country. It just floors me how so many 'religious', 'Christian' people forget that while Jesus had a lot of time and respect for his elders, he had little time and no respect for the self-righteous"

"Well said. I know that prolifers are getting more active but road rage is on the rise too and I won't stop driving so..." Lynda said.

The two friends chatted happily for a couple of hours, exchanging news and bits of gossip.

When Lynda returned home, there were three calls on her answering machine but no messages.

Lynda mentally shook herself, saying, "Now I'm just being paranoid" as she deleted the record of the calls, all with blocked caller-ID, which she tried not to notice.

The rest of the day was happily uneventful as she unpacked from the weekend, did all the laundry, and did some writing. Sean came home from school solo. Lynda was a little surprised. She asked him, "Isn't Karen coming over for dinner?"

"Doubt it." Sean's shoulders were slumped and he walked up to his room without elaborating. Lynda was dying to know what had happened but forced herself to leave him be.

Half an hour later the doorbell rang. Lynda answered the door doubting that Sean had even heard the chime because his music was so loud. Standing before her was a furious ball of energy in the form of Karen. Her body was taut and her fists kept clenching and unclenching.

"Hi, Mrs. B.," Karen said, "Is Sean home?" Her voice betrayed the tight rein she had on her anger.

Lynda stepped aside and waved Karen inside. "Follow the music."

Karen marched in and went straight to Sean's room. A few seconds later Lynda heard a loud and demanding knock. She held her breath and prayed that everything would work out all right.

Sean turned down his music and opened the door. On seeing Karen before him he was stunned speechless. He just stood there, staring at her with his mouth gaping open. Karen brushed passed him and entered his lair. Sean closed the door behind her. His mind was working so fast it seemed to have ceased functioning at all. There was so much he wanted to say but he never thought he'd get the chance and now his tongue was incapable of working.

Karen turned to face him. She was stunning in the middle of his room with her hands on her hips and her eyes flashing dangerously. "Well?" was all she said.

Sean tried to speak, really he did, but muttering was all that emerged.

Karen pushed hard on his chest and made him stumble backwards. 'How could you?"

"I'm sorry. I didn't exactly say anything, you know." That's right, his deluded adolescent brain told him, defend yourself. "Besides, you said you didn't care what people thought." His voice was almost smug.

Karen's jaw fell open. "And you believed me!" Her eyes started to tear and she turned away. She would not let Sean see her cry. She couldn't believe she had almost trusted him with her secret, how could she have been so stupid. She was so glad she hadn't told him! At least she had that.

Sean's stomach lurched. He felt wretched. He had no idea how to fix this. The whole day at school had been excruciating. He kept getting pats on the back and smiles and thumbs up from every guy he knew and many he didn't. He'd seen Karen too. The girls were whispering and giggling, turning away from her as she walked by with her head held stubbornly high. Only Maddie had talked to her at all. "I'm so sorry Karen," he said and he was. He felt like an ass.

Karen felt the truth of his words. She hugged herself as she stood there with her back to him trying desperately to stem the flow of tears. Despite her best efforts her shoulders began to shake. Sean moved closer to her and tried to rest his hands on them comfortingly but Karen jerked away and turned to face him. Seeing her tear stained face made Sean unable to breathe.

"I trusted you! I thought you were different. I thought I really meant something to you."

Sean reached out to her again but she backed away. "God Karen, don't you think I would do anything to undo it."

"Why would you? Your reputation is set."

He groaned in response. "I was a coward okay? I was weak. I didn't want to be seen as the only male virgin left in high school."

"Especially if you could've been with me. I mean how lame would that be, not to be able to score with me, right?"

Her accusation stung because it was true. "Tell me what I can do. Anything please! Karen I don't want to lose you."

She laughed a mirthless laugh. "You know, the truth is, this is worse than the other rumors because I didn't see it coming. But you are no different from every other guy who has ever used me. We're done Sean. We are so done." With that she turned and left. She never even said goodbye to Lynda, she just left.

Michael came over for dinner as usual. He and Lynda chatted and laughed throughout the meal trying to compensate for Sean's sullen mood.

Then the phone rang. Lynda was still chuckling at Sean and Michael's antics when she picked up the receiver.

The line was quickly disconnected.

"Must be a wrong number," she said.

Lynda started cleaning the table and, just as everyone got up to help, the phone rang again.

Another hang-up.

Everyone seemed to stop in mid motion and exchange glances.

Michael put down his plate and took the phone from Lynda's hand, hung up, and dialed *69.

When he hung up he shook his head. "No luck. The call-return feature cannot be used to return your last incoming call," he said, mocking the voice of the recording.

Lynda looked at him. "Should we take it off the hook?"

Michael thought for a moment. "No, one more call and we call Detective Hughes."

"But I thought they couldn't really do anything?"

"We'll just see about that. Putting all these calls together—Susan's, mine, and yours—ought to be enough for them to do something."

Silently the three people cleared the table, each waiting for the next call, each wondering what it all meant.

Ring! Lynda jumped. Michael answered the phone.

"What?"

He heard a sharp intake of breath, and then nothing. He immediately hung up and dialed Susan's number.

It rang once, then twice, and again a third time. "C'mon, pick up." It rang a fourth time, but time was moving slowly.

Then finally, "H-h-hello?"

"Susan, hi, it's Michael."

"Hi."

"Listen, I need Detective Hughes' phone number."

"Why?"

"Lynda's getting calls now."

"But surely that has nothing to do with us," Susan said indignantly.

"Just get me the number please. We'll let him decide what's related and what isn't. I'm not taking any chances." Michael was furious. And afraid. He looked at Lynda; her eyes were huge and wary. She blinked and regained her composure. She turned to Sean and put her hands on her hips and, in a mock cop voice, said, "Nothing to see here, folks, move along now."

Sean said, "Okay, Mom. I'll be around if you need me."

She smiled. "I'm the mom, you're the kid, remember?"

"Whatever," Sean said, in imitation of an '80s preppy teenager.

Lynda let herself laugh and flicked at him with a dishtowel as he made his way to his room.

In the meantime, Michael had hung up from Susan and was calling Detective Hughes.

She turned to Michael as he hung up the phone.

"Well?"

"He's on his way, but he's not sure there is anything he can do."

"He's coming here, now? We'd better clean up." Lynda got busy loading the dishwasher and wiping down counters.

Michael watched her. He ached to hold her and make this all go away. But he just stood there, studying her tense little body.

When she put the sponge down and looked up at him, she was struck by his look of indecision. She went to him and they held each other.

"I wish I could make this go away," Michael said.

Just then the doorbell rang.

"Let's go," Lynda said.

Just as Lynda was pouring the last cup of tea for the three of them, the phone rang again. Lynda turned to Detective Hughes, questioning him with her eyes as to what to do.

"Put it on speaker," he said. He took out his notebook and noted the time.

A deep, slightly distorted voice said, "Someone like you doesn't deserve to be a mother." Click. The phone disconnected.

Lynda was pale and shaking as she picked up the receiver and hung it up.

Michael turned to Detective Hughes. "Well, now we know it's connected to the clinic. Can you do something?"

Detective Hughes sighed. He scratched his head, thinking.

"Well," he paused, "I will look into this, but phone stuff takes time, and technically the caller hasn't threatened Mrs. Blake."

"What?" she snapped, "I sure as hell feel threatened."

"I'm sure you do. I think, though, that you are not in any real danger. The callers we worry about are the ones who are very explicit."

Michael jumped in, "But if this is the same person who called Susan and me, surely this is a pattern of harassment! And how did they get our unlisted numbers?"

Detective Hughes nodded. "That's an important question. I think, given the unlisted numbers and now the comments made to Mrs. Blake, I can get the DA to expedite any phone search, but first we have to get a trap on your phone and hope for another call tomorrow. I'll do all the paperwork and call the phone company myself."

Lynda looked at him. "So you really can't get the info like they do on NYPD Blue and CSI?"

"Afraid not, but I'll do the best I can, ma'am. I am taking this seriously."

"Do you think my son is in any danger?"

"Probably not."

"Never have I disliked the word 'probably' more," Lynda said. She looked at Michael. Was "probably" good enough? She closed her eyes and sat down. She felt nauseous. She'd survived losing David. She knew she couldn't survive losing Sean or having him hurt, especially if she could have prevented it. When she looked up her decision was written all over her face.

Michael's heart sank. He wanted to argue with her, he wanted to fight. He started to reach out to her.

She held up her hand to halt him. She whispered, barely audible, "I can't risk losing him or having him hurt."

Michael stopped. His arm dropped to his side. He couldn't ask her to. This was crazy and out of control. With tears in his eyes, he kissed her cheek. He said, "I won't ask you to," then he turned and walked away.

Detective Hughes wanted to say something but it was too soon; there simply wasn't enough evidence for him to be sure, so he held his tongue and said nothing. He just watched Michael walk away and Lynda stiffen before his eyes.

After Detective Hughes left, Lynda took a deep breath and did what she did best. She carried on. She put one foot in front of the other. She walked up to Sean's room. She knew he needed her even if he didn't. She knocked on his door.

"Come in," Sean said.

So she did. She saw him at his desk with his notebooks open. Lynda ached to hold him and take all the sadness from him, but he wasn't two years old anymore. A Mommy hug couldn't fix everything. So instead she sat on his bed. Sean turned around in his chair to face her.

"So," he said, "What's the deal?"

"They don't really know."

Silence. Then Lynda began. "Seems like you had a rough day."

"Mmm."

Silence. "Nothing is ever easy, is it?"

"Nope."

"I'd like to help, if I can." She prayed to God and Mary that he would let her in and that she could help her son. Hadn't he already hurt enough in his young life?

"I don't think you can, Mom. I screwed up. Big. And sorry just isn't enough."

Lynda sent another quick prayer heavenward that she could find to right words. And in a flash she remembered one time in high school when a boy Eric had courted her, giving her flowers every day in the week leading up to Valentine's Day. He didn't care if people teased him; he wanted everyone to see how much he cared about her. Lynda smiled at the memory.

"Have you thought about doing a big, public, somewhat embarrassing apology and display of affection? Nothing tells a girl you care like doing something you know the guys will rag on you for. It's really romantic."

Sean cocked his head sideways and thought. "Not bad, Mom, thanks."

Lynda stood up to leave. "Good luck sweetie." Since he was sitting down she was able to go over to him, take his face in her hands and kiss him on the forehead. She turned and left her son to his work.

The next day at school Sean waited until lunchtime to put his plan into action. He wasn't going to give Karen up without a fight. Strangely enough, as embarrassing as this was going to be, he might just get his self respect back, even if he didn't win Karen back. That was the real reason he had the courage to do what he was about to do.

He went to his car to get his sports duffle bag and returned to the foyer in front of the cafeteria. People were settling in to their usual places by now, having found their friends and congregated according to the ancient social rules found in the high school world. The jocks were together and raucous; the popular girls preened and lorded it over everyone else. All the various cliques had assembled and were laughing and chatting in their well-defined spaces. Sean surveyed the scene and gulped.

Man, there really were a lot of people here, he thought. He spotted Paul and Maddie and Karen on the edge of the foyer. Paul was looking somewhat put out because Maddie had her back to him and was focused on Karen who was looking like she was trying to look like she felt normal and it was taking an extreme effort. Paul spotted Sean and waved him over. When Karen saw him coming she stood up to go but Maddie held her arm.

"Don't let him chase you away. He can go somewhere else." She turned to Paul, "Right Paul?"

Paul scowled at his girlfriend but before he could say anything Sean said, "Karen please don't go." His eyes held hers intently, begging her to stay.

Karen stayed standing and crossed her arms in front of her but she didn't move. Sean put his bag down and knelt to open it. He pulled out a single long stemmed red rose and from his knees he offered it up to her. Maddie gasped and covered her mouth with her hand. A ripple of elbows and pointing and whispers swept through the room. All eyes were on Sean and Karen.

"Please," Sean said, "Please forgive me. I am so sorry."

Karen quickly glanced around the room. She looked back at Sean; he was still on his knees holding the rose out to her.

"Stand up," she hissed at him.

"No," he said clearly. "Not until you forgive me." With one hand he reached back into his bag and pulled out a stuffed animal for her, a cute little donkey. He held it up to her with the rose. Girls all around the room 'Aaahed'.

"Please," Sean said gently wiggling the stuffed donkey, "I know I was an ass."

Karen giggled and accepted the rose and stuffed animal from him. "Okay," she said, "But don't do it again." She'd give him another chance but she wasn't sure she could forget.

Sean exhaled audibly, letting out a huge breath of air he hadn't realized he'd been holding. "Thank you," he said standing up. He bent to kiss her. As their lips touched applause and cheers rose around them and Sean and Karen laughed and blushed together.

"You really were an ass, you know?"

Sean grimaced, "Do you honestly think I would have humiliated myself like that if I didn't?"

That night Karen was back over at Sean's house for dinner as usual, though she hadn't come home straight after school with Sean. She'd said she had something to do first. Lynda smiled and thought that at least things were mostly back to normal for one of the Blake's. That night as she lay in bed she thanked God for her son, for his happiness and for his safety. She prayed for the strength to carry on alone because all of a sudden it seemed so much harder than it had before she'd met Michael. She knew she could do it, she just prayed that it wouldn't hurt this much for too long.

Chapter 14

A very long week later Lynda called Detective Hughes. She told him that she hadn't received any more calls and asked if things had calmed down for Michael and Susan too. He assured her they had, and added that he was not off the case but to be realistic, there was little more he could do at this point.

Lynda hung up, relieved that the danger seemed to have passed for everyone. It was probably just one of those things after all. Lynda was unconsciously pacing in her room after she put down the phone. Despite relatively vigorous and physically satisfying workouts, her pink bunny vibrator just didn't measure up to the real thing. She missed Michael. She missed the smell of him, the taste of him, the feel of him. Lord knows she'd been productive enough lately. Writing had been tough, but when she couldn't create she got her editing done. At night she'd gotten caught up on her scrapbooks but that didn't exactly distract her because she didn't have any pictures of Michael to put in there and that just felt wrong.

Sean and Karen came home a few minutes later and looked at her as she greeted them with a forced smile in her voice and on her face.

"Hey you guys, how was school?" They were all in the kitchen as usual. Sean needed to raid the fridge the moment he got home. Lynda was passing him a glass to make sure that he wouldn't drink straight out of the carton.

"Mom," Sean said, concerned. "Enough is enough. Call Michael."

She just shook her head. She hadn't told him about the threatening call, just that the detective had said they "probably" weren't in danger, and that wasn't good enough.

Karen studied her, and Lynda crossed her arms, trying to shield herself. All week Lynda had been wearing sweats. Her feminine, but casual, Chico's boutique look had disappeared. "What is it, Mrs. B.? What haven't you told us?"

Lynda's eyes flashed to hers.

Sean looked from Karen to her mother. "Mom? Is there something you haven't told me?"

Lynda bit her lip, took a deep breath, and said, "You'd better sit down."

They all moved to the kitchen table and sat.

"The last call, the one I got when Detective Hughes was here, wasn't a hang-up."

"It wasn't?" Sean said.

"No, a distorted voice said that I didn't deserve to be a parent."

Karen inhaled audibly. "Oh my God."

"What did the detective do?" Sean said.

"Well, technically it wasn't a threat, so it wasn't a felony, but he put a trap on the phone and we hoped for another call, but it's never come, so he can't move forward."

"Not like TV, huh?" Sean said.

"No, criminals have lots of rights in California. The phone company won't give any information on calls not on phone traps, and even then tracing them can take a week to ten days, especially if the phone comes back to a throwaway cell phone. Which, if this nut was able to get unlisted numbers and a voice-distorting mechanism of some sort was what they probably used."

"So that leaves the cops nowhere basically," Sean said.

"Pretty much. But the calls have stopped at least and apparently things have quieted down for Michael and Susan and the clinic too."

"So you talked to him?" Karen said hopefully. She was looking quite beautiful today, without wearing anything special. Her jeans and top were both casual and showed off her figure without drawing undue attention to it and yet she was riveting. She had become more comfortable with who she was and it showed.

"No, Detective Hughes told me."

"Oh."

Sean looked at his mom closely. "So that's it?"

"I guess so."

"Mom …" Sean was exasperated.

"What?"

"C'mon. Call Michael."

She shook her head. "No."

Sean turned to Karen, beseeching her for help.

Karen simply said, "Tell us why, Mrs. B. You obviously miss him."

Lynda smiled sadly. "How can I call him? What about the next time? What if a real nut job goes after you, Sean? I can't put you at risk, put me at risk of losing you. I won't."

Sean walked over to his mom. He hugged her. Would she ever get used to the fact that he towered over her?

"Mom," he said quietly, "you're not going to lose me." He put his hands on her shoulders and looked her in the eye. "You miss him a lot. You should call him. You are punishing him and yourself and you're letting the bad guys win. Whatever happened to fighting the good fight? I remember 9/11, Mom. I remember how you and Dad made it a point to travel after 9/11 because you wouldn't let the terrorists win by changing the way you live. But now you are letting terrorists dictate who you choose to be with."

Lynda sighed. "There's a big difference between 9/11 and now, Sean. We weren't specific targets then."

Sean turned to Karen. "Can you help me here?"

Karen looked at Sean and Mrs. B. She took her time before responding. "No, I don't think I can. I mean, I wish your mom and Michael would get back together too, but she won't go back to him. Not while she thinks you might be at risk."

Exasperated, Sean threw his hands up in the air and practically shouted, "But I'm not at risk!"

"Probably," Karen agreed, "but right now 'probably' isn't good enough for your mom and who can blame her?"

"Aaah! You're making me want to go out and get a motorcycle and ride without a helmet!" he said, referring to an old promise he'd made that he'd never ride a motorcycle while he lived under his mother's roof.

"Moving out early, are you?" Lynda said.

"No. But wait a minute, if you'll let me get a motorcycle when I'm living on my own, will you call Michael and see him when I've gone off to college in the fall?"

Lynda opened her mouth as if to speak, but nothing came out.

"Well?" Karen said. "It's a fair question."

Lynda smiled relenting. "Yes, it's a fair question. Okay, I'll call him when you're safely off at college, but," try as she might she couldn't hide the ache in her voice, "you realize he'll probably be seeing someone else by then ... "

Sean grinned mischievously.

"Oh, stop looking so satisfied with yourself!"

Karen laughed at the smug look on Sean's face. He could be as much of a meddler as his mother was. She was sure he was up to something.

Lynda looked a little flustered and didn't seem to see what Karen saw, which was probably just as well. Sean and Karen soon headed up to his room to do homework. When Karen and Sean were alone up in his room, Karen finally asked, "Okay, spill. What's your plan?"

Sean was standing at his desk getting out his books from his backpack, playing coy. "Plan? What plan?"

"Puhlease." Karen had thrown her books on Sean's bed and made no pretense of settling down to work.

Sean laughed. "Okay, okay. I figure if Mom plans on calling him in a few months anyway ..."

"Closer to ten actually."

"Details. Then he should know that she's going to call and maybe we can move up the timeline a bit."

"You mean a lot."

"Yeah, well, the first step is to visit Dr. Michael."

"And just when are you planning on doing that?"

"How about tomorrow, after school? You in?"

"Absolutely," Karen said.

So the next day after school, Sean and Karen headed over to the Women's Clinic. When they walked in, Susan was at reception with her head down, focusing on paperwork or something despite the controlled chaos of the waiting room.

"Excuse me," Sean said politely. "May we please see Dr. Cameron?"

"Do you have an appointment?" Susan said, looking up.

Karen quietly studied her, remembering how Maddie had described her. She was chic, cold, and slightly smug or rather, very smug, and hiding it as best as she could.

"I'm afraid not," Sean said, "but we'll be happy to wait."

Susan nodded and passed him a form to fill out. "All right. Bring this back to me when you've filled it out."

Sitting in the waiting area Sean turned to Karen. "What do you think? Do we fill it out?"

"I don't know. Let's look at it."

It was a standard form. They filled in her name and address and basic health history and left it at that. When Sean brought the form back to Susan, she took it and noted down Karen's name in the appointment book and asked Sean for his name and noted it down. Then she looked at him and down at his name in the appointment book and back up at him, a furrow lining her brow.

Karen couldn't help herself. "I think you've met Sean's mother, Lynda," she said helpfully. "That's probably why he seems familiar." Her voice was syrupy sweet.

Susan's eyes darkened, but she forced the furrow out of her brow as she said evenly, "Oh, that must be it." But her cockiness had wavered momentarily and Karen thoroughly enjoyed that!

Returning to their seats, Sean said, "Nice."

"I thought so."

The office was busy and they had to wait quite a while. They managed to get much of their homework done as they waited. Eventually Susan brought them back to Michael's office.

When he read the name on the file Michael was both nervous and happy. He was anxious for news of Lynda but in truth, Karen and Sean were probably here about birth control or something, and it wouldn't be appropriate to ask about her. He realized he was standing outside the door stalling. Shaking his head at himself, he opened the door.

"Hi Sean, it's good to see you, and Karen too, of course." He shook both their hands and motioned them both to sit back down as he sat behind his desk.

"What can I do for you?" he asked. He looked questioningly at Sean, then back to Karen. She surreptitiously shook her head no in answer to his unasked inquiry about whether or not Sean yet knew about her past and if that was why they were there.

The two teenagers looked at each other and grinned.

Karen said, "In for a penny, in for a pound."

Sean nodded.

Michael watched the two of them carefully. He leaned back in his chair. Something was up.

"Well," Sean began, "you see, it's like this. Umm, but first, well … do you miss my mom? And I don't mean just a little."

Michael's eyes grew wide. This is not what he expected. "Yes, I miss her. More than I ever thought I could, if you must know." He was annoyed and curious too. He let the curiosity dominate. "What's up? Why are you two here?"

His answer satisfied Sean and he continued, "She misses you too. A lot." He waited for a reaction from Michael, who simply nodded.

"The thing is, I got her to say that she'd call you when I was off at college."

"Oh."

"The problem is that's not till next fall."

"I see."

"So I want you to call her."

"What?"

Karen jumped in. "We figure if you just call her casual-like, to see how she's doing and let her know everything's fine at the clinic … "

"How do you know everything is fine at the clinic?"

"Detective Hughes told her when she asked him the other day."

"She asked him about me?"

"Of course she did," Karen said. "She's been worried about you. She's just still worried about Sean, that's all."

Michael shook his head. "I don't know. I can't very well ask her not to worry about you. Nothing's changed, not really."

"Except you're both miserable and I'm fine. Just call her. Tell her we came to see you. Tell her something. Open the door."

Karen said, "Let her take baby steps back to you. It's what she wants to do."

Michael chewed his lip for a second, and then stopped. There were two very determined young faces before him.

"But what if she gets more crank calls?"

"Maybe this time she'll believe they are just calls."

"I don't know. She's scared. She has a right to be. I'll think about it."

Sean looked directly at Michael and said seriously, "Don't give up on her. She's lost a lot. I don't want her to lose you, too."

"I can't promise anything, but I will think about it."

"Please," Karen added, "think hard."

He nodded as he led them out of the office. And think about it he did, but he couldn't decide what to do.

In the days and weeks that followed, the office was busy and Susan was putting in lots of overtime, working on strategies to raise their profile in the community and developing plans to increase the size of the practice. Michael went along with it because it kept him busy and her happy. Actually deciding whether or not to implement the plans would come later. For now, he'd rather work late at the office than go home to a quiet, empty apartment. But try as he might, he couldn't forget about Lynda, or Sean or Karen for that matter. He missed them a lot, but he wasn't about to give up his practice for them. He longed to talk to Lynda, to hear her voice.

"What are you thinking?" Susan asked in an almost sultry voice.

He started when he realized just how close she was to him. He had to stop his mind from wandering.

"Oh, nothing much," he answered unconvincingly.

"Mmm?" Susan rested her hand on his shoulder. "I've really enjoyed working with you the last couple of weeks. Feels like the good old days."

Michael got up and walked out of reach as he went to file some paperwork. "But it's not the old days, Susan."

His bluntness surprised her and it showed.

"It could be, if you let it, you know. I've learned a few things since I made the biggest mistake of my life leaving you."

Michael's shoulders sagged. He didn't want to deal with this. "Susan, I ..."

She walked over to him and put her finger to his lips to silence him.

"C'mon Michael, we could be friends with benefits." She kissed his lips lightly. "I know just how you like it."

He put his hands on her shoulders and pushed her away. "No, Susan, you don't. I've changed too, and I don't want to go backwards at this point in my life."

"So let's move forward."

Michael felt cornered. He couldn't believe Susan's relentlessness. Where was her pride?

"Susan. You're not listening to me."

"That's because you're not saying what I want to hear. I know if you just give me another chance I'll make you happy."

"No, Susan. No. I won't pretend to feel something for you that I don't. I would just be taking advantage of you, and that's no way to treat a friend."

"I wouldn't mind. You might change your mind, you know."

Michael wanted to scream in frustration. But this was his fault. He had been taking advantage of her to keep busy with work while he missed Lynda. He wasn't really interested in expanding the business. He just wanted a nice, manageable practice. All of a sudden this seemed too familiar.

"Sometimes I'm not a very nice person," Michael said. "I'm sorry, Susan. I truly am. I'm going home." He grabbed his jacket and stormed out of the office, disgusted with himself, leaving Susan surprised and perplexed in his wake.

Chapter 15

A couple of weeks, later things were more or less back to normal at the office. Michael had quashed the expansion ideas as nicely but as firmly as he could. He had stopped working late with Susan. When he wanted to avoid going home, he went to the local YMCA to work out. This seemed to be happening at least four times a week and the results were beginning to show. A little more definition was appearing in his arms and abs, but he had no one to show them off too. He either didn't notice or didn't care to notice any of the encouraging glances sent his way by other shapely bodies coated in a light sheen of sweat that were working out alongside him.

Susan took the change in plans pretty hard. She pushed, nagged, encouraged, and tried everything she could to bring Michael around to her way of thinking. In the end, he let her redesign their brochure, reorganize their distribution plan and formalize their outreach to schools and medical practices, but that was as far as it went.

She kept trying to spend time with him at lunch in the office, but he did his best to be elusive. Towards the end of the second week, she suddenly started giving him his space and being somewhat elusive herself.

Michael tried not to act relieved around her, but in truth, that was exactly how he felt. He was planning to head up to his place in Sonoma that weekend. He finally felt ready to be there again. He was getting used to being alone. Not that he liked it much, but it was better than using someone else to get his mind off of Lynda. At least he could respect himself this way. He still longed to call Lynda, to hear her voice, to taste her lips, to … if he kept going like this, he'd never get anything done.

He knew he was going to need a few things for the weekend, so even though it was ten o'clock at night, he headed out to the grocery store. Why he chose to go to the one closest to Lynda's house was something he didn't want to analyze. No one likes to feel pathetic, he reasoned to himself; therefore it must be the great produce section that drew him there.

He was nervously choosing some fruit when, for the first time in a long time, the fates smiled on him. Lynda came in through the sliding doors. She looked tired, tense, and more beautiful than he remembered.

She picked up a small basket by the door and headed left, away from the produce straight towards the frozen foods.

"Lynda?"

She stopped dead in her tracks, spun on her heel and faced him.

"Michael!" There he stood flesh and blood before her. He looked amazing—taut, fit and fabulous enough to eat.

She seemed genuinely happy to see him. That both encouraged him and made him more nervous. "I'm picking up a few things for my ride up to the vineyard this weekend."

"How is Serge?"

How is he, Michael thought—how am I?

"He's fine. He really took to Sean. How is he, by the way?"

Lynda thought, isn't this all very safe and polite? "Sean's doing fine. He and Karen are still going strong."

"I know."

She looked at him, puzzled. "You do?"

"Yeah, they came to see me several weeks ago."

A million thoughts raced through her mind. Well, not a million—actually, just one. They either were going to have sex or were having sex already. Her feelings about that were intense and definitely included more than a little panic.

Seeing her face pale Michael quickly said, "No, no, they didn't come to see me as patients; I wouldn't tell you if they had. No, they came to ask me a favor."

"Oh." She chewed her lip in that especially endearing way of hers, trying to figure out what she could ask balancing Sean's right to her trust and his privacy versus her curiosity and need to know. "Is it anything I should know about?"

Michael smiled at her. Nothing ventured, nothing gained, he told himself. "Why don't we finish our shopping and I'll buy you a cup of coffee and tell you the whole story?"

"Okay," she agreed. "I'm just on an ice cream run. I won't be a minute."

Michael was humming to himself as he quickly chose a few plums, decided that was enough for now, and met Lynda in the checkout line.

"What flavor did you get?"

"Cherry Garcia, my favorite pick-me-up." The words were out before she could censor herself. Her eyes flashed in horror. Had she actually just admitted to using ice cream as her own personal anti-depressant? Would he assume that missing him was the cause of her need for sugar and fat?

Michael enjoyed her disquiet. He couldn't resist teasing her. "Should I take that as a compliment?" His voice was cocky and arrogant.

He got a quick jab to the ribs in response. He laughed, a deep, rich, infectious laugh, and Lynda laughed too.

As they left the store Michael asked, "Should we take one car or two?"

"Um, would you mind swinging by my place so I can put the ice cream in the freezer? Then we can go in your car, if you don't mind dropping me off afterwards."

"Sounds like a plan."

Ten minutes later Lynda was settling into Michael's Jag. It didn't take long for her to wonder if being in such a confined space with him was such a good idea. Her body practically hummed in awareness of Michael's proximity. She couldn't help but notice the way his trousers strained against his strong thighs and she had to force herself not to look any higher.

He was just as attracted to her. If he didn't distract himself and fast, Lynda's gaze would see all too clearly just how much she affected him.

"So where are we headed?" he asked, his voice more strangled than he would have liked.

"I don't know. This town is dead after nine, but there must be something on El Camino."

Michael nodded and turned on the radio. They both focused on the jazz as they drove around looking for a late-night coffee shop. Fifteen minutes later Lynda sat with her head back and her eyes closed, relaxed, having decided to just go with the flow.

Michael hit the steering wheel in frustration. "I can't believe that I can't find a place for a decent cup of coffee."

Lynda chuckled softly. She opened her eyes and looked around. "We're not too far from your place, let's just go there."

Michael literally gulped. "Um ..."

"Don't worry, I'll be good. I promise not to jump you."

He groaned, "Well, that's hardly good news."

Lynda laughed, relaxed. She was tired, really tired.

Michael looked at her closely. She looked beautiful and exhausted. "Maybe I should take you home."

"Mmm, not yet. I've missed talking to you, you know."

"Me too."

A few minutes later they pulled into the parking lot of Michael's townhouse. He put his arm around her as they walked to the door. She snuggled right into him and he felt a surge of protectiveness for this woman. He opened the door without loosening his grip on her. He escorted her to the sofa, then went to the kitchen.

"Do you want coffee or tea?"

She yawned. "Do you have any decaf black tea? If I have any caffeine now, I'll never get to sleep."

"I've got your favorite tea here. You look like you could use some sleep, Lynda."

"Mmm. I've been trying to catch up, but I've been having a hard time falling asleep and an even harder time getting up. I try not to nap so I'll sleep better at night but some days I just can't keep my eyes open."

Michael brought in two mugs of tea.

"Two sugar and milk?"

"I remembered," Michael said.

She smiled. "So what exactly did Sean and Karen come to see you about?"

"You." He said it so simply, so directly.

"Oh. But you didn't call."

"No."

"Michael, I am ..."

"It's okay."

"I am so sorry about everything. I'm not sure I could have done it any differently, but I am so sorry I hurt you."

"I know you are. I know you got hurt too. The kids told me the calls stopped."

"Naturally." Her voice betrayed her rage. She forced herself to take a deep breath. "Listen, I didn't call because Sean is still in the line of fire. As much as I hate letting the bad guys win, I won't put my child at risk so I can be with the man I love. That hasn't changed. And it won't until he is safely away at college. And I can't ask you to wait. It's not fair. I hate it, but there it is. I have to be his mom first, no matter how much I love you and miss you and want to be with you."

"You know it was just a crank."

"I don't know that and frankly I don't think so. I think it is someone smart and determined. Cranks can be dangerous too, you know. God knows I'd love to be wrong, but I don't think I am."

Michael sighed. "You did tell me you were stubborn."

She grinned slightly and nodded.

"Well, I guess I'll just have to wait then."

Lynda guffawed.

"What?" he asked.

"Michael, you can't do that."

"Watch me. I can be just as stubborn as you are."

Then she smiled. "I truly hope so." She yawned in spite of herself.

"C'mon, woman, I better get you home."

On the drive back to Lynda's, Michael replayed what Lynda had said over and over in his mind. She didn't think the caller was a crank. What if she was right? But she had to be wrong, didn't she? Or was that just wishful thinking? Maybe he should call Detective Hughes next week and find out what he thinks.

He parked in front of Lynda's house. She'd been awfully quiet on the ride home.

"We're here," he said, turning to her.

She was sound asleep. She looked peaceful and content and, for now, he had to let her go. He walked around to her side of the car and opened the door. He unbuckled her seatbelt and she barely stirred. He chuckled to himself. He was actually going to have to carry her inside. When he picked her up, she sighed and snuggled into him. His heart swelled with love for this fierce mama bear who needed him to carry her to bed.

When he got to the door he had to ring the bell for Sean. Sean came to the door surprised and delighted to see Michael.

"She's out like a light."

Michael carried her up to her room, lay her on her bed and lamented that he could do no more than tuck her under the covers. She murmured something incomprehensible as he left her room.

Sean was waiting for him downstairs.

"Well?"

Michael grinned with resignation. "I have to be a very patient man, but I won't give up on her."

Sean shook his head. "She won't budge at all? But she let you take her out."

"We bumped into each other and had a cup of tea together. That's all until you are safely off at college where some lunatic targeting the clinic won't be likely to bother you."

"Man, I'm sorry."

"Don't be. She wouldn't be her if she wasn't an over-protective Mom. It'll be okay. We'll work it out." He hoped they'd work it out. He had waited his whole life to find her. Now that he had, he hated their spending even one day apart.

Sean said, "You know she loves you, right? She didn't sleep for like two weeks after you guys split, and now I find her crashed out on the sofa at all hours. Maybe things will get better now that she's talked to you."

"I hope so. Listen, if you need anything, or if your Mom does, call me."

"Okay, but we'll be fine."

"I know you will. But it's kind of hard that I need you guys so much and you don't need me."

In a moment of teenage wisdom, Sean said, "But Michael, now we know we've got you, that's why we're gonna be fine. Mom will relax and wait."

"Thanks."

"Don't sweat it."

And with that, Michael drove home. Alone.

Chapter 16

A week later, Lynda was still exhausted. She felt like her whole body was off. Frustrated with herself, she finally called her doctor. She did some research online first, so that when she called Dr. Tina's office she asked to have an appointment to get her thyroid checked. They squeezed her in just before lunch.

Tina had wanted to see her first before ordering the blood test. She was sitting on the exam table yawning when Tina came in.

"Hi Lynda. I see you want your thyroid checked?"

"Yeah, I'm dragging and I have a strong maternal history of hypothyroidism, which is the good kind, right? The kind where I get a pill a day for forever and I'm fine."

"Yeah, I will be happy to test your TSH. According to my notes we tested you six months ago at your physical and it was fine, but that doesn't mean it isn't starting to act up. What else is going on besides being tired?"

Lynda thought for a moment. "Well, my digestion is acting up. I can barely eat before noon. I've gained some weight, I think; my pants are getting snug at the waist. I know that your metabolism slowing down is a symptom of hypothyroidism but I didn't see anything about the digestion thing."

Tina asked a few more questions about hair loss—no, late menstrual period—yes, both of which are also common symptoms of hypothyroidism.

"Queasy?"

"Yes."

"Are you sexually active?"

"Not at the moment. I broke up with my boyfriend a couple of months ago," to which Tina arched a curious eyebrow.

"The boyfriend's new," commented Tina. "Sorry it didn't work out. Did you have unprotected sex with him at all?"

Sheepishly Lynda nodded. "Once."

"Shall we do a thorough STD and HIV screening?"

Lynda sighed embarrassed. "That's what I'd make Sean do. So yes, let's go ahead and do that."

"While we're at it, let's do a pregnancy test too."

Lynda snorted. "Isn't that overkill, Tina? I mean, I was never able to get pregnant after Sean, and I'm hardly at my most fertile."

"Well, what could it hurt? We'll do a quick urine test and have the results before you leave."

"Whatever you say, Doc."

"Okay, you wait here a sec. I'll get one of our deluxe specimen jars and we'll do the pregnancy test here while you go to the lab for the blood tests. Then you can come back to my office."

Twenty minutes later Lynda entered Tina's office and perched nervously in a chair facing Tina's desk. Tina never ran unnecessary tests. What if she was pregnant? She was too old. She was almost done raising Sean. What about Michael? What about her? This was crazy! It had to be her thyroid, it just had to be.

Tina walked into the office and smiled at Lynda.

"Tina, you've got me totally freaking out here. I'm not pregnant. I can't be pregnant. Can I?"

"Take a deep breath, Lynda."

"No, just put me out of my misery. Tell me I'm not pregnant."

Tina looked sad. She sighed, "You know we have come a long way in pregnancy testing. The tests you can get in the pharmacy are just as accurate as the ones we use here. We don't need to do blood tests anymore. It is usually a relief to get the results so quickly."

"Are you stalling?"

Tina actually blushed a little. "Sorry, I guess I am. Lynda, you are definitely pregnant."

Lynda's jaw fell open and she slumped back in her chair.

"Lynda, you do have options, you know. We can talk about them."

Lynda waved her off. Tina waited.

"I'm old, Tina, in my forties, that makes me high risk, doesn't it?"

"Yes, but a good risk given you've had a healthy child already. I would like to make an appointment for you to meet with Dr. Mitchell Barnes right away."

"A guy?" Lynda rolled her eyes.

"If I were in your place, he'd be my first choice. He's the best."

Lynda reluctantly nodded her assent. "Okay, set it up."

A moment later she looked up, panicked. "Oh my God. I haven't been taking folic acid or any of that stuff. I've forgotten all about being pregnant. What do I do?"

Tina reached over and squeezed Lynda's hand. "It'll be okay. You'll figure it out. In the meantime I'll write you a prescription for prenatal vitamins. Take them on a full stomach. Take a deep breath. Go meet with Barnes and try to figure out what you want to do. It's still early, you know. You've got some time."

Lynda just shook her head. "Not really. Not unless something is really wrong with the baby. Otherwise I'm having her … or him. I'm grown. I can afford it. And for me it just wouldn't be right not to."

"Okay."

"You seem a little surprised, Tina."

She shrugged. "As long as I've known you, almost 18 years, you've been pro-choice, and clearly this is an unexpected pregnancy. I'm just surprised you're so clear about what you're going to do."

"That's the thing about choice—I get to choose what's right for me. I shouldn't get to choose for someone else."

"I think the politicians forget that there are a lot of us who choose life for ourselves as being right, but don't judge or choose for others. Lynda, I'll be here all the way through, whatever happens. You'll need to talk to Barnes about early ultrasounds and CVS, amnios, family history and risk factors. Let me call his office now. He works out of the Women's Center up in Port Valley."

Tina called and got Linda an appointment for 8:30 a.m. the next day. Lynda left the office in a daze, praying to God that nothing was wrong, even though nothing was quite right.

At 8:00 the next morning as Lynda was heading out the door, Sean said, "You're off early today."

"Yup. I have a doctor's appointment."

"I thought that was yesterday," Sean said, scratching his head. As unobservant as teenagers could be, he couldn't miss that his mom wasn't herself. He'd been a little relieved when she'd said she was going to something checked yesterday.

"I did. They want me to see a specialist." Well, it was true, she thought to herself.

"Are you okay?" Sean was starting to worry.

"Fine, they just want the right department dealing with the right problem, but that doesn't mean it's a big problem. This is just routine." She hated hiding the truth from him but she wasn't yet prepared to discuss her situation with anyone. She didn't want Sean to worry, though.

Sean looked at his mom, really looked. She was trying her best to look relaxed. He tried his best not to let her see him worry. That would only make her stress more and tell him less, trying to protect him. He knew his mother very well.

When he talked to Karen at school about it, they thought a quick chat with Dr. Michael might enlighten them a little. So after school they went by his office.

Susan didn't seem all that happy to see them. Just after she had told them it would be a long wait, Michael poked his head around the corner.

"Thought I heard familiar voices. Everything okay, you guys?"

Karen spoke up. "We think so. We have a quick question we're hoping you could answer."

"Sure. Come on back to my office. I'll be with you in about fifteen minutes."

Sean and Karen smiled with saccharine sweetness to Susan as they walked past.

After Michael sat himself behind his desk he looked at Sean and Karen. "Okay, what's up now?"

Karen looked at Sean encouragingly.

Sean said, "Well, Mom's still really tired and she went to her doctor to get her 'roid' or something I think checked, and now she's off to a specialist. She told me not to worry, and I don't want her worried that I'm worried, if that makes any sense, so I came to you to see if you know anything that can help me."

Michael smiled. "I'm sorry she's still run down. She probably had her thyroid checked and now they've sent her to an endocrinologist. All perfectly normal. If she has hypothyroidism, which is diagnosed through simple blood tests and is extremely common, her endocrinologist will work with her to find the right dose of medicine and she will take a pill every day for the rest of her life, and that's it. This is very common in women your mom's age."

"So nothing to worry about?"

"No, not if it's hypothyroidism."

Sean sat back and exhaled. "But why wouldn't she just tell me that?"

"Probably the same reason you came to me instead of talking to your mom. Do you want me to check in with her?"

Sean looked to Karen.

She said, "Well, it couldn't hurt, could it," with mischief in her voice.

Sean nodded.

"Okay, you two, enough of that. But I will give her a call just to make sure she's got a good endocrinologist."

"Sure, that's the only reason," said Sean.

"I'm a patient man. I never knew that before, but it turns out I am."

The implication was understood by all who heard it. Just then Susan knocked on the door to his office.

"Patient in exam two is waiting for you."

"Gotta run. See you guys later." Michael got up and headed into the hallway toward his patient.

"Thanks, Susan."

"I didn't realize you were still involved with Lynda."

"I'll always be involved with Lynda. I love her."

Sean and Karen couldn't help but overhear. They left the clinic with hearts much lighter and happier than when they'd entered. Just as they closed the clinic door behind them, Susan came out.

"You kids be careful now," she said.

They turned to her, puzzled.

"See that guy in the Mazda?" She pointed to a car in the Albertson's parking lot.

"Yeah …"

"That's Ron Thompson. He's been watching the clinic all day. The police can't make him move because he hasn't done anything yet. I'm worried he might be photographing people coming and going to the clinic." She turned and went inside.

For a minute Karen didn't say anything.

"If the police already talked to him," Sean began, "then he can't be photographing people, can he?"

"Probably not," Karen agreed. "Still, it's spooky."

"Yeah, but …" Sean was thinking as they drove away. "I mean, he can't have been there all day. That's loitering, right? I mean he was in a business parking lot, not at a park. Susan must be a little over-sensitive after all the trouble they had last month."

"Who can blame her? I'd be freaked too, getting crank calls to my brand new unlisted phone number," Karen said.

"It was nice of her to watch out for us," Sean said.

"Yeah, it was," Karen agreed. "I'm just glad Michael's not giving up on your mom."

Sean smiled. "Me too." He put his arm around Karen. "I want her to be as happy as I am."

Karen just smiled. She was happy too. She didn't want to say or do anything to ruin it. She loved Sean and she knew that he loved her. She knew she'd have to tell Sean eventually about her father sexually abusing her, but she didn't have to do it yet.

After dinner that night Shelley called Lynda just to catch up.

"Let's go out for a drink," Lynda said.

"Okay," Shelley said, a little surprised. "Meet you at The Grill?"

"Great, thanks Shell."

Lynda needed to talk to someone, and who better than her best friend in the world. She called up to Sean in his room that she was going out for a drink with Shelley.

"I won't be late."

"'Kay, Mom. Have fun."

The Grill was a local place with a huge bar in the middle and lots of tables and booths along the sides. The volume was always loud and the service friendly and swift.

Lynda got there first and somehow managed to snag a table right away. She sat facing the entrance and ordered herself a cranberry and Sprite. When Shelley came in, Lynda waved her friend over. Shelley sat down and ordered herself a Cosmo and waited for her drink to arrive. Lynda was awfully quiet and wouldn't quite meet Shelley's eyes. When the waitress left she took a sip, smiled and put her glass down.

"Okay, Lynda, what's up?"

Lynda squirmed in her seat. This was harder than she thought. She took a deep breath, squared her shoulders and blurted, "Would you believe I'm ... pregnant?"

Shelley choked on the second sip of her Cosmo. "No!"

Lynda nodded sheepishly.

"Oh my God! When did you find out?"

"Yesterday. I saw a high-risk specialist today and learned about CVS and amnios and percentages. My mind is a blur."

"I'll bet. I don't even know what a CVS is."

"It's a prenatal diagnostic test, Chorionic Villus Sampling, I think. They take CV cells that are of fetal origin. It can detect Downs Syndrome, which is important. I'm at 1/100 risk factor for that because of my age, but it also tests for Tay-Sacks, Sickle-Cell Anemia, CF—or most kinds of it, anyway—and a bunch of others. They only test for stuff other than Downs if there is a family history of it. The good thing about it is that they can do it early, at 10-13 weeks, and the results take 7-10 days, unlike an amnio, which they do at 16-18 weeks and the results take 3 1/2-5 weeks."

Shelley, sitting very still, just stared at her. "Oh."

Lynda shook her head and slumped her shoulders. "I'm too old for this, Shell. I've forgotten it all."

"Apparently not."

"Please, I didn't need to know any of this with Sean. I breezed through that, assuming it would be all right. Now I have a one in one hundred chance of having a baby with Downs."

Shelley reached for her friend's hand. "I'm here, you know."

Lynda nodded. A tear rolled down her cheek.

"You don't have to do this, Lynda."

Lynda smiled sadly. "Yeah, I do."

Shelley took a deep breath. "Does Michael know?"

Lynda shook her head no.

"Are you going to tell him?"

Lynda chewed on her lower lip. "I want to wait until after the CVS at least, maybe after the amnio. I mean, if something comes up that I decide I can't cope with then maybe he never needs to know if I … if I … Oh God, I can't even say it. Short of the baby not being viable, I'll find a way to cope with whatever comes." She sighed. "Shelley, I'm going to have a baby."

"I know. So about telling Michael?"

"What about Sean? I won't sacrifice him for a baby that's not even here yet. Maybe I can wait till Sean's away at college. Oh Shelley, Sean's going to be in college and I'm starting over with sleep deprivation and being velcroed to another human being!"

Shelley waited a moment. "So about telling Michael?'

Lynda looked at her. "Are you trying to tell me something?"

Shelley arched her eyebrows in response.

"I'll tell him. I will, but I have to keep Sean safe and this baby too." Lynda looked down.

"Lynda, stop right there! You are not thinking about keeping this baby away from its father, are you?"

"I don't know. I don't want to. Michael would be an excellent dad. But …"

"No, Lynda. No buts. Hire bodyguards if you want, but you know you have to let Michael in, and now. All the way in to your life, not second place behind the kids. Remember what you told me years ago. The best thing parents can do for their kids is to love each other."

"Oh, sure, throw my own words back in my face! But what about Sean? Do you think he'll be okay?"

"Oh Lynda, I wish I could say for sure that you're being over-cautious. I think you are, but maybe you need to have a frank conversation with the detective who dealt with the harassing phone calls."

"That's a good idea, Shell."

"Thanks. But, once Sean's safe, you have to let Michael in. You know, part of me thinks that, as much as you miss him, a tiny part of you was relieved that you didn't have to really love him and commit to him, to risk needing him and then be left alone again."

Lynda's first reaction was to think no, that's crazy, but Shelley knew her very well. She forced herself to think about what Shelley had said. Finally she looked at her best friend and said, "I'm not sure. I mean, I don't think so, but I can't rule it out entirely. Maybe I am overreacting to the phone thing more to protect myself than to protect Sean. I just don't know. I can't shake my gut feeling that it was real."

Shelley finished her Cosmo and shrugged her shoulders. "I don't know what to say, Lynda. Your gut has never steered me wrong, but our need to protect ourselves can be overwhelming too. Just think about it, okay? And whatever you do or don't do, I'll be here for you. I can figure out diapers and formula again!"

"Thanks." She paused. "Another round? I don't want to go home yet."

"Okay. What are you having, by the way?"

"Cranberry juice and Sprite. Ah, being on the wagon and giving up my body begins!"

The two friends laughed together. They ordered another round. Lynda was more relaxed but still not at ease.

"Shell, the real question is when do I tell Sean?"

Their drinks arrived, giving Shelley a chance to think.

"Well, he's not your typical teenager. He grew up a lot after David died. But I'll bet he won't figure it out on his own for a while. You could wait until the end of your first trimester if you want." She sounded hesitant.

"I sort of lied to him. I let him think I have a thyroid problem, which is what I thought I had before I found out."

"Mmm. Well, is your guilty conscience going to give you away? Do you think he'll understand your not telling Michael right away?"

"I just don't know. I have no idea how he'll react. I think I will take you up on your earlier suggestion and talk to Detective Hughes first, then I'll probably call you again and then go from there."

"Okay. At least now you have the beginnings of a plan."

Lynda nodded. Changing the subject she said, "Would you believe I can barely close my pants? My waist has ballooned about a size and a half already!"

Shelley laughed. "There's more where that came from!"

"Don't I know it!"

The two friends chatted and joked for another half hour before saying goodnight. Lynda hugged her friend tightly. "Thanks, Shell. Thanks for everything."

"That's what I'm here for."

The next day Lynda dropped by the police station. It was hard to believe that her tiny town had such an amazing police department; they had several K-9 units; car, motorcycle, and bicycle cops; a SWAT team; state-of-the-art communications; a ton of community outreach programs; and more. All of a sudden Lynda didn't mind her property tax bill quite so much. As luck would have it, Detective Hughes was in and available. Armed with doughnuts and coffee she met him in a conference room.

"Hi Lynda. What can I do for you today?'

She smiled. It was hard not to feel safe and scrutinized at the same time.

"I guess I'm really looking for a dose of perspective."

He nodded silently, waiting.

"On a scale of one to ten, where did the threatening call I received rank, honestly?"

"About a one or two at the most."

"I see." She paused, not sure exactly where to go next.

"Do you think the calls would start again if I got back involved with Michael and, if so, how worried should I be about that?"

Detective Hughes thought very carefully before he spoke. "There is always a chance they will start again. If I had to guess, I'd say 60-40 they will. But as to how worried you should be, that depends on a lot. Like whether or not the calls escalate, especially in terms of specifics. The call you received was, in my experience, someone trying to scare you. The calls we worry about are ones promising explicit, specific violence or other crimes."

She thought about what he said. "But there's no way to predict whether or not the calls will escalate?"

"No, there isn't, but the statistics are on your side. Even if they do, we can trace the calls because we have a trap on the line. If you're considering getting back involved with Michael, I'd suggest not letting anyone—not even him—know you still have it. There might even be something to be gained by letting people think that the time on the trap ran out and, since you didn't get any other calls, you let it go."

Lynda sat very still. She watched and listened to Detective Hughes closely. She felt there was something he couldn't say to her and she tried desperately to hear what it was. "Can I ask you something else, Detective?"

"Sure."

"As a police officer, you must have made a number of truly nasty people very unhappy over the years. Has your family ever been in harm's way as a result?"

He leaned back in his chair and exhaled. "No, but it is something we have to worry about from time to time."

Lynda nodded. "Thank you so much for your time and your candor. Please keep the trap on my phone. I'm not sure what I'm going to do yet, but it'd be nice to have it just in case."

Detective Hughes stood and shook her hand. "Sure thing. Thanks for the coffee and doughnuts," he said, only now taking one. "Keep me posted, will you?" His voice was casual but his eyes were deadly serious.

Chapter 17

During the next few days Lynda had little time to consider what Detective Hughes had said, because she was hugging the Porcelain God morning, noon and night.

"How can I have anything left to throw up?" she moaned to herself, as she crawled back into bed. "This has to be psychosomatic! This has to end soon!"

The front door clicked closed behind a quiet Sean and Karen. Lynda could hear them moving around downstairs. She forced herself out of bed, splashed water on her face, put some track pants on and headed down to the kitchen.

Sean took his head out of the fridge to say hi to his mom. "You're not feeling any better?"

"I'm not feeling any worse."

Karen looked at Lynda, looked closely. Lynda forced herself not to squirm.

"This is quite a long bout of the stomach flu, Mrs. B. Are you staying hydrated?"

Something in Karen's voice made Lynda uneasy. "I'm trying, thanks."

Lynda turned around to make herself a cup of tea. She hoped Sean would miss the undercurrent of tension between her and Karen. He almost did. He might have, but Karen nudged him.

"What?"

Karen just looked at Lynda and arched her eyebrow.

"What?" he whispered.

"Look at her, doesn't she look different to you?" she whispered.

Sean looked at his mom. "Uhh, no."

"Sean," she whispered, exasperated. "She's gained weight despite throwing up for three days. She's been tired for weeks."

"I know. That's the hypothyroidism. I looked it up online. It slows the immune system so you catch more bugs. It slows your metabolism so you gain weight. It's all normal," Sean said in a normal voice.

Hearing this, Lynda's shoulders slumped. She took the tea bag out of her cup and threw it away before she turned around.

She wished she was relieved that she could hide behind the hypothyroidism, but she wasn't. She felt guilty. If Karen had figured it out, she should tell Sean now, not later, and pray he understood about not telling Michael right away.

"Sean," she began as she cupped her warm and soothing cup of tea to her chest and leaned against the counter for support, "Karen's right. I don't have hypothyroidism, although that is what I thought I had, and they did do a test for it." She paused. She took a deep breath. "I'm, well … I'm pregnant."

Sean's jaw fell open. "Mom?"

"I know it's a shock. Believe me, it was a bigger shock to me."

"Are you okay?" Karen asked.

"Sort of."

Sean just stared. The horror on his face was unmistakable. "I need some air," he said. "I am going for a walk." He turned to Karen, "I'd appreciate the company."

Karen just nodded and the two of them silently left the house. Lynda stared at her hands for a moment, took a deep breath, then began tidying up the house, rearranging things that didn't need rearranging, for the most part.

Half an hour later Sean and Karen returned. Sean tried hard to use the right tone of voice when he spoke to his Mom. He knew this was an important conversation but his insides were still far from calm at her revelation.

"Mom, what are you … where's Michael? Did he bail on you?" Sean's mind was racing. He wasn't sure where to start.

"Let's all sit down, okay?"

They did.

"To answer your first question, the one you couldn't quite bring yourself to ask, I'm planning on having the baby. True, I'm old, but I'm in good shape and barring anything drastic I'm going to have the baby."

Sean stared at his mom. "Okay," was all he said.

"And as to the second question, I haven't told him yet. I will, but not for a while."

"What?" Sean was indignant. "Why?"

Lynda was obviously struggling to find the words; her eyes darted around as she thought. She looked truly pained.

Karen said, "Is it because you are worried about the crank calls, that if you get back together with Michael then Sean will be in danger?"

Sean turned to Karen, then back to his mom. She nodded.

"Oh, but what about Michael?"

"The baby won't be here for a long time. I'll wait as long as I can, as long as I have to."

"Mom, you are way overreacting."

She sighed. "Don't you think I've considered that? I went and saw Detective Hughes a few days ago, you know. There's a chance the calls will start again, and they did escalate from hang-ups to verbal harassment. Who knows where it will go from there?"

"Mom, you're being ridiculous. Nothing is going to happen to me."

"Why, because you're immortal?" Her voice became agitated. This was so hard for her. Why couldn't he see her point of view? "You are my child. I will protect you as long and as well as I can." Lynda sat, tense and taut.

"Whether I want you to or not?" Sean's voice was getting louder too. "Mom, you need Michael now more than ever!" Karen touched his arm, silently willing him to calm down.

"I'll be fine. If everything comes back fine from the CVS tests, then I'll think about telling him then." Lynda said tiredly.

"When's that?" Sean asked, softening slightly.

"A couple of weeks, a month at the most." Lynda waved her hand vaguely.

"The results don't take too long."

Sean relented.

"But," Lynda said firmly, "if anything happens that makes me think you'll be in danger, all bets are off until you're away at college. I promise I won't keep this baby from her father, but I will do whatever I have to do to keep you and her safe."

"Her?" Karen said.

Lynda shrugged. "Or him, but maybe her."

"I'm going to be a big brother!" Sean said, somewhat amazed. "I'm going to be a big brother and, if I go away, I'm going to miss everything."

"So don't go too far!" Lynda said, "But go. Otherwise you won't sleep at all for your freshman year."

Sean thought about that. "Okay, but I want to go somewhere I can be home on weekends, so I can get to know my little sister or brother."

Happy to change the subject, Lynda said, "I thought you'd want to come home for weekends to do laundry and get real non-cafeteria food at least once a week."

"That too!"

They all laughed. Lynda looked at Karen and asked, "What about you, Karen? Where do you want to go next year?"

Karen said, "I'm waiting to see who gives me the most scholarship money and loans. I don't want to be in debt forever for going to school."

"I hear that," Lynda agreed.

"Do I need to worry about money, Mom?" Sean asked.

"No, that's my job, but your dad and I planned for this, so you'll be fine. I do expect you to help with money from summer jobs, of course."

"Of course," Sean said. "Why do I suddenly feel spoiled?"

"Not spoiled, Sean, but very lucky," Karen said.

"I would say privileged," Lynda said, "And as you know, with privilege …"

"Comes responsibility," Sean finished.

"Your dad expected, as do I, that you take your classes seriously, do your assignments and homework on time and ask for help when you need it. Not so outrageous, is it? Maybe not always easy, but definitely fair."

Sean walked around the table to his mom and kissed her on the cheek. "Don't worry, Mom."

Karen smiled, then got teary.

"Karen, my dear, it is unwise to get teary around a pregnant woman," Lynda teased gently. "What's wrong?"

"I just look at you two and you are this close family like on TV, you know, and …"

Lynda reached out and touched her hand. Sean went to her and said, "And it's not like your family, is it?"

She just shook her head.

"But at least your mom wouldn't sleep around and get pregnant when she's old!"

"Hey!" said Lynda, as she and Karen simultaneously and playfully, slapped him.

He laughed.

"Thinking about family, you think Dad'd be bummed if I don't want to go to Harvard?"

"There's always grad school; that's when he went, anyway."

"Gee, Sean, no pressure!" Karen said.

"No, none at all," he agreed.

Lynda looked at him startled and surprised. "Is there a lot of pressure from me? Is it too much?"

"No, Mom, not really. In a way, it's been good knowing that going to college is my next step. As for where I go and the Harvard thing? It is a lot, but probably more because Dad's gone than if he was here."

"Wow, that was insightful. You know what he wanted most was for you to get a good education and work on things you love and to be happy."

"Yeah, I know," Sean said, "but I want to make him proud, you know."

"I know. You do, Sean, you already do." Lynda closed her eyes and sent up a quick prayer to David and to God that Sean really did know how proud David must be of him, that Sean could still feel David sometimes, like she did.

Karen jumped in. "All right, you two, you are going to make me cry, again! I never even met your dad, and I already like him way better than mine." She paused. "Do you think he would've liked me?"

Sean said, "Definitely."

Karen turned to Lynda. She had asked a serious question and from the look on her face wanted a serious answer. "Well, yes, once he got to know you he'd love you as much as I do, but it might have taken him a little longer to open up to you at first."

Karen nodded. "Okay I'll take that. You always keep it real, Mrs. B. Thanks."

Lynda nodded.

"I think this is more than enough heavy stuff for one day, you guys, don't you? Besides, I suddenly feel a need to go out for chocolate chip ice cream. You guys want to come?"

Sean's eyes twinkled with mischief. "Not if you're gonna have pickles with that."

Lynda laughed and Karen groaned. "Not today, Son, but I'll keep you posted."

Sean turned to Karen, wondering if she wanted to go, and she answered with a barely perceptible incline of her head. She had been craving some family time and they were the closest she had to a real family.

After they were all loaded in the car, Lynda looked in the rearview mirror and saw Sean and Karen together. "I feel like a chauffeur!"

"I feel like we're being chaperoned!" Sean retorted.

"Please tell me you don't need a chaperone!"

"Not as much as you do, apparently!"

They all cracked up.

Lynda relaxed. If Sean was teasing her like this, then he really was okay with the pregnancy. That was a big load off her shoulders. Now she definitely needed some ice cream!

When they pulled in front of Lappert's Ice Cream store, it was surprisingly busy. As they got out of the van, Lynda heard a familiar voice that put her on edge. Susan was there holding a baby, rather stiffly, but trying to be relaxed.

"She's just beautiful, Carol," Susan said.

"Thanks," the woman responded.

Then Michael's head popped up, seemingly out of nowhere. "She really is adorable." He turned to a man standing next to Carol and said, "How are you guys doing now that she's a bit older? Is she sleeping more?"

The man nodded and smiled. "Life started getting better when she was around four months. That's when she learned to put herself down to sleep at night. She's eight months old now and it's a lot more fun." He smiled at his daughter in Susan's tense arms.

Lynda checked the clock on her cell phone. It was barely 5pm. She tried to decide whether or not to say hi, not wanting to intrude, afraid Sean would spill the beans. She itched to have Michael's eyes turn toward her, with love and desire at the sight of her. Before she could decide, Sean piped up.

"Hey, Michael, Susan, what are you guys doing here?"

"Sean, hi. Hi, you guys," Michael said to Karen and Lynda. He looked surprised to see them. "We're having an impromptu staff and family ice cream social. Let me introduce you to my nurse, Carol, her husband Ron, and their little Betsy."

With the introductions made, Lynda felt her heartstrings tug. She practically ached to hold Betsy.

"May I hold her?" Lynda asked Carol. "Please, it has been so long. Sean is already seventeen. It's happened so fast."

Carol smiled. "Of course. Go ahead."

Lynda thanked Susan for handing her over. Susan didn't seem overly thrilled about the hand-off, but Lynda was beyond caring once she held little Betsy and smelled that special baby smell. Lynda started cooing and talking to her, rocking her like an experienced mom. It was all coming back.

Michael stood riveted, watching her.

"Looks like you're a pro," Carol said.

"I guess it all comes back." Lynda was beaming. She glanced at Michael and saw the longing he was trying to hide. She smiled warmly to herself.

Susan turned to Lynda and said, "I bet you can't imagine ever having another baby, can you, with Sean almost grown and all."

Her eyes not leaving Betsy, she said, "Actually, I've been thinking about it a bit lately."

Sean elbowed Karen as she coughed to cover her laugh. Michael's gaze turned to utter perplexity.

"Umm, Mom, why don't we get our ice cream now?"

"Okay," she said, reluctantly handing the baby over to Carol.

Inside the store, Karen said to Lynda, "Mrs. B., were you trying to give Susan a heart attack back there?"

In her best mock maternal voice she answered, "Now Karen, that really wouldn't be nice now, would it?"

To which they both laughed and Sean said simply, "Women!"

Once they were back outside, Lynda finally asked what had prompted the staff family ice cream party.

Michael groaned and Susan almost crowed. She said, "The anti-choice activists trashed our clinic last night. It was impossible to work today; just reorganizing the files and washing the walls took most of the day."

"Oh my gosh, was anyone hurt?"

This time it was Carol who answered. "They are pro-life, Lynda. It is their job to harass and intimidate, but not to harm."

Lynda thought about that. "You've got a good point. So you don't worry about Betsy at all?" Lynda absentmindedly rubbed her belly ever so slightly.

"No," said Carol.

"Sometimes," said Ron.

Susan's eyes flickered with light. Carol and Lynda looked at Ron. Lynda held her hand still on her belly then forced it to rest casually to her side.

"What? I worry about you too sometimes, but you wouldn't be you if you did something else. And I know statistically you are probably more likely to get hit by a car than hurt at the clinic, so I just deal with it."

Michael spoke up. "Well, I for one am sick of these anti-choice activists. I've already hired a top-notch consultant, Mac, who'll help us totally redo the clinic security and evaluate each of us for our personal security needs. So don't worry, Ron, I am doing everything I can to keep Carol and Betsy and all of us safe."

"Thanks," Ron said seriously.

Michael nodded in response.

Susan was silent. Sean nudged his mom, and she shook her head in response. She had just taken her last bite of ice cream and, as she threw her cup away, she said goodbye to everyone and smiled warmly at Michael, but that was all.

In the van Sean said, "Mom?" impatiently.

"Not now, Sean. I need some time, at least until after the first round of tests."

"Coward!"

"Whatever!"

Chapter 18

ichael watched Lynda drive away. He was confused and distracted with having to host his employees and the fallout from the crazy day. He wanted to chase after her but he felt trapped. Susan was yammering something at him; he really ought to pay attention. Forcing himself to focus, he turned to Susan, realizing for the first time that she had looped her arm in his.

"I'm sorry, what?" he said, trying unsuccessfully to discreetly disentangle himself. Sighing, he relented and left her arm looped through his. He still hadn't heard a word she had said. How could one woman so completely enthrall him? He was so frustrated he wanted to curse Lynda and absorb her all at the same time.

"Well, Michael, what do you think?" Susan asked happily.

He looked at her. Damn it, he still had no idea what she'd said. He looked to Carol for help.

She smirked ever so briefly and said, "Well, Ron, Betsy and I can't go out to dinner tonight. We've got to get the little one here home; maybe some other time?"

"Oh," said Susan, trying to sound disappointed, "what about you, Michael?"

Smiling quickly at Carol, he said, "Sorry Susan, I can't tonight, but we should schedule a night for all of us to go out soon. Carol, let me know when you can get a sitter and we'll work around that. Okay guys?"

Michael successfully moved away from Susan and was saying goodbye when his cell phone rang. He looked at the caller ID and said, "See you guys later. I've got to take this."

He headed to his car as he answered the phone.

"Michael here."

"Michael, Mac here." His voice was cold, clear and efficient. "I wanted to report on what we've found out so far. A pro-life group online, one Ron Thompson is affiliated with, reporting on the assault on the clinic. They are not claiming responsibility, but they have too many details, if you know what I mean."

"Go on."

"We've done a preliminary check on all your employees and, as you suspected, we've come up blank, but we're still working on the employees of the cleaning company, your electricians, plumbers, and so on. We'll keep you posted. If we have to do detailed checks, that could take a few weeks. I've talked with Hughes and am keeping him in the loop."

"Good, thanks."

"The new security cameras and system should be installed and operational within a week; until then we'll have someone on site 24 hours a day."

Michael sighed. "Sounds good. I'm trusting you with my people, Mac. Thanks for moving so fast."

"It's what we do."

"And as for personal security needs of my staff?"

"It would be peace of mind only. You are the only real target and you don't need much beyond good security at the clinic right now. If that changes we'll deal with it then."

"Okay."

"I'll be in touch." And with that, he rang off.

By now Michael was sitting in his car. The others had all left and he breathed a huge sigh of relief. If he had to mortgage the vineyard to pay for this, it would be worth it. This was the right thing to do for everyone. This might even be enough to get Lynda off her schedule of waiting until fall when Sean was away at college. Lynda, sweet confusing Lynda. Had she really said she was thinking about babies? Did she just say that to get to Susan? God, it had been one hell of a day.

As he turned on his car and put it into drive, he knew exactly where he was going. He wondered if she knew he was coming.

When he pulled into her driveway, he parked and just looked at the house. It was a brown split level with a wood shingle roof, the birch trees in the front corner of the yard were full and delicate, the flowers he couldn't possibly name were blooming in quiet colors, muted oranges and reds. The lawn was trimmed but not manicured. It was nothing special or different from any other house on the block and yet it was. It was easy to see it was a home. It was her home, Sean's home, probably Karen's too, for that matter. It was going to be his home too; he just had to be a little more patient and persistent.

He knew he should have felt tense as he walked up to the door, should have felt nervous and unsure of his reception, but he didn't. He felt calm—calm and confident.

When Sean answered the door, Michael was pleased at the teenager's reaction. Sean said, "About time. She's in the kitchen eating again." Then he motioned to Karen to come over and called out, "See you, Mom. Karen and I are heading out for a drive then we're going to hook up with Paul and Maddie for a movie."

"Okay, be careful, have fun," came the reply.

At the door, Karen looked at Michael, then at Sean. She took a deep breath and caught Michael's eye as she quietly said to Sean, "Yeah there's something I've been meaning to talk to you about, privately." Michael smiled and nodded at her encouragingly, then stepped inside to go find Lynda.

The two teenagers sat in Sean's car in the driveway talking for quite sometime. In a quiet voice Karen told Sean everything about how her father had begun sexually abusing her at he age of ten, how it had started as touching and quickly escalated to his raping her on a regular basis until her period started when she was thirteen. Sean held Karen as they both cried for what had happened to her. His body radiated anger. He's never felt so much of anything in his life until now.

"Let's go and get out of here for a while, okay," Sean said to Karen. He felt so helpless as she dried her tears and tried to smile at him. He had to protect her, to help her somehow. He couldn't believe what she'd told him but he knew it was true. How could anyone hurt such a beautiful child, see any child like that? He just didn't understand it. Karen had really taken a chance and trusted him. He could feel in his core what that trust meant and what it had cost her to expose herself like that to him. He felt so many things, honored at her trust, disappointed that it had taken so long for her to really trust him and also that, somehow, his childhood had just ended. The world was different to him now and there was no going back.

"Sounds good to me. Let's go. Thanks for listening, Sean. I've been seeing someone about this, you know, when I disappear after school for a bit on Wednesdays. Michael hooked me up with a therapist after I talked to him the night when we went to his vineyard. I just need to know that you don't see me any differently." Her voice got small and quiet, like a child's, "That you don't think I am dirty or damaged goods or something."

Sean looked at her in horror, 'Oh God Karen, of course not!" He grabbed her and held tight in his arms. "How could you think I'd think that? I love you. I want to kill your father for what he did. But the sin is his not yours, Babe, it is not yours. I love you so much. I just want to make sure he never hurts you again. That nobody ever hurts you again." They cried together a little more. "I wondered what you were doing after school those days but somehow I knew I wasn't supposed to ask. Thanks for telling me." Sean started the engine of his little Honda and they headed off to drive, just drive. They both needed a break from life for a little bit.

Meanwhile, Michael headed into the kitchen. Lynda had her head in the fridge. She hadn't heard him come in.

"Hi," he said, his voice deep, relaxed, full of love.

She jumped in surprise and banged into the fridge door. Her heart raced. She longed to hold him but, if she did, she was afraid he'd feel the changes in her body. He'd know.

"Hi," she said, as she backed away, rubbing her elbow where it had connected with the fridge. She walked to the opposite side of the island from him. "I'm so sorry about the clinic. You must have had a horrendous day."

Michael shrugged in response to her words but her actions left him concerned. He needed to hold her but she was moving away from him and yet she seemed happy to see him. "Yeah, but at least now I've got professionals working on the security."

Lynda's eyes shone with the rush of conflicting emotions and thoughts. "So you said. Do you want a cup of tea or a beer or something? And you can tell me all about it."

A few minutes later they were sitting opposite each other at the kitchen table and Michael was filling her in on all the details of the day. When he was done he leaned forward across the table and took both her hands in his. "I'm doing everything I can to make it safe for everyone."

She looked down. Feeling the warmth and strength of his hands on her, made her skin tingle. She wanted so much more. Maybe she should just tell him. Before she could make up her mind, Michael said, "There was something else I wanted to talk to you about."

"Mmm," she looked up, grateful for the reprieve. Why was she so afraid to tell him, to turn that corner to forever? "What's that?"

He let go of her hands and sat back. He looked at her closely. As he spoke his voice wavered just a bit. "This afternoon you said you'd been thinking about another baby. Was that just to irritate Susan or was it true? Are you thinking it might be a possibility?"

Lynda searched frantically for the right words. "Well, as much as I enjoyed shutting Susan up, the truth is if it happened I wouldn't run from it."

Her words were measured and careful. He wasn't sure what he had expected her to say. She seemed on the verge of elaborating when the phone rang.

Lynda cursed herself as a coward as she went to answer the phone. "What? I can't hear you!" she yelled.

"Mrs. B.! ... road ... car ... "

It was Karen and she was scared. Her cell was going in and out. "Someone is ... ass... off ... road!"

"Where are you?" Karen yelled into the phone.

"Up ... Page Mill ... near ... line."

"Hang up and call 911 right now!"

Michael was by her side.

"We've got to go!"

"What's going on?"

"That was Karen. She and Sean are being run off the road. She said something about Page Mill near Skyline I think! Her cell signal wasn't great."

"Damn it, that's a dangerous stretch of road. Let's take my car. You call 911 too just in case she couldn't get through."

The roads up there were nothing but blind curves and switchbacks with virtually no shoulder for safety.

*   *   *   *   *

Behind the Honda, only one car length back, the big black SUV loomed.

"Hang on, Karen!" Sean cried as he whipped around the next corner. The shuffle steering his mom had forced him to learn was finally coming in handy. Sean dutifully kept his hands low on the steering wheel with his palms facing him. He kept his eyes looking ahead to the next turn he would need to take. He maneuvered the car quickly, turning the steering wheel minimally. He let the car do most of the work. That's what his Mom had always told him, "Let the car do most of the work. It will go where your eyes go if you let it. Most people way over steer." Time and again, she repeated to him, "They over drive and end up with their arms all crisscrossed over each other and then they have to let go of the wheel all together. In an emergency that is just too dangerous." She'd harped on him to always be a safe driver, always be a smart driver, and, "Then you won't become a statistic."

"What the hell is going on?" Karen cried.

"Can you see who it is or get a plate number?"

Karen tried to turn around and look but was slammed back into her seat as they tore around another corner.

"What do we do?" Karen asked.

"Pray." Sean was grateful his eight-year-old Honda Accord was handling well.

"I already am."

The trees were whipping by on their left and the cliff was ever present on their right. The light was starting to fade; the shadows were growing across the road.

"I think there's a pullout in about a mile. I'll try to get out of this idiot's way!" Sean yelled. His palms were sweaty and his pulse was racing. Beads of sweat were dripping from his forehead into his eyes but he was afraid to take his hands off the steering wheel to wipe them away. His eyes never strayed from his ever-changing focal point. He'd never driven so fast around these corners before. The cliff was there just daring him to err.

As the tiny pullout appeared at the side of the road, Sean slowed and signaled his intent. He was afraid to hit the gravel shoulder going too fast. The pullout spot was small with no guardrail to speak of and the cliff was waiting for disaster. The cliff was literally one side of the San Andreas Fault Line.

Sean was about to turn into the gravel pullout when the black SUV rammed into them from behind.

"Shit!" Sean yelled as the car fishtailed. "You okay?" He kept the nose of his little Accord pointing where he wanted the car to go and it came in line quickly.

"Yes!" She was grabbing the holy-shit bar above her window for dear life. "If this is it for us, I wish I'd made love with you before now!"

"Now you tell me! What if we make it?"

"After I finish kissing the earth I'll jump you, I promise!"

"Promises, promises," he teased.

The SUV rammed them again.

"Son of a bitch! Who is this nut job?"

"You just worry about driving, okay?"

The intersection of Page Mill and Skyline approached rapidly.

"Turn right on Skyline. There's a restaurant you can turn into and stop!"

"Okay, but get a good look at the car as they pass. Hang on!"

He didn't brake, and he could feel Karen tense. He took his foot off the accelerator a heartbeat before he yanked on the parking brake hard. Both back wheels locked up and they skidded straight for a fraction of a second before Sean looked around the corner and turned the steering wheel ever so slightly. The tires squealed as the rear of the car raced around the corner. With precision befitting a stunt driver, he released the parking brake and tore down Skyline and turned into the restaurant parking lot. The black SUV tried making the corner but instead did almost a 360° turn and rocked on its wheels as it came to a stop. The driver turned the vehicle around and followed them down Skyline Boulevard.

The SUV sped past the restaurant. Moments later they heard sirens far in the distance. Sean was breathing hard. His hands shook as he turned off the car. They unbuckled their seatbelts and were about to get out of the car when Karen looked in the mirror on her door and yelled.

Sean whipped his head around to see the black SUV return. The driver was wearing a baseball cap and mirrored sunglasses. Sean pushed open Karen's door and shoved her out of the car just as the black SUV rammed into the car again, pushing it to the edge of the parking lot near the cliff.

Karen hit the ground and rolled away from the cars. "Sean!" she yelled.

Why wasn't he out? "Sean!"

She stared in horror as she watched the car go over the side of the cliff. The world seemed still until she heard the car crash to a halt.

It was the laughter that made her vomit, but not before she got some of the license plate etched into her brain. She ran to the cliff. Nothing seemed to make sense! The driver of the SUV was still laughing as it raced away. The sirens were much louder now, but all Karen could see was Sean's car motionless at the base of the trees and overgrown shrubs almost 300 yards down the cliff face. It was so still! She sobbed but no sound came out. Her whole body heaved as she tried to breathe. She fell to her knees and rocked back and forth.

That was how the police found her. An officer put his coat around her shoulders. He spoke to her but she couldn't hear him. She said, "Black SUV," and pointed in the direction it had gone.

The officer looked at her and she gave the officer what little she had of the plate number and promptly threw up again. She said, "Laughing, they were laughing when they killed Sean… He saved me… Pushed me out of the car." The officer muttered into the radio on his shoulder. Two officers worked their way down to Sean's car. Karen heard another car pull in to the restaurant and looked over at it.

Michael and Lynda looked at the chaos of the parking lot. Lynda jumped out of the car as it stopped. She saw Karen and ran to her. "Are you okay?" She nodded.

"Where's Sean?"

Karen's tears finally started to flow. All she could do was point.

Lynda could see the tracks over the side. Two officers were halfway down to the car. She chased after them. An officer tried to stop her, but it was too late.

"Ma'am, you can't go down there!"

"The hell I can't!" She ran and scrambled adeptly down the hill, surprising the other officers as she swiftly passed them. She ignored their shouts and twisted away when they tried to stop her.

The first thing she noticed was that the car was full of a white dust. That meant the airbags had deployed. She prayed they had done their job. He had to be all right. He had to. She had to believe life wouldn't be this cruel to her. As she got to the driver's door, she saw Sean slumped over the steering wheel, not moving. He was just unconscious, that had to be it. Dear God in heaven, that had to be it.

She tried to open the driver's-side door but the tangle of brush made it hard. She turned to the police officers and screamed, "A little help, please!" She was furious at how long they were taking. My God, she thought, why can't they go any faster? In reality they were being incredibly efficient, even given the first-aid kits and equipment they were carrying. They quickly reached the car, though it seemed an eternity to Lynda and forced the door open. The two officers exchanged unreadable glances.

"Don't move him!" yelled Michael, running down the hill. "I'm a doctor. Don't move him until I check his neck and back."

Karen was making her way down the cliff behind Michael.

"He's got his seatbelt on," one officer said to Michael.

"But how?" Karen said. "We had our belts off before they pushed him over the cliff."

Lynda was talking to Sean. "Mom's here, baby. Just relax. Michael's going to take care of you. All you have to do is wake up, sweetie."

Michael was at Sean's side by this time. "He has a strong pulse, no difficulty breathing."

The officer told Karen, "He must have gotten his seatbelt back on somehow, because he's wearing it and it may just have saved his life."

"He's alive?"

Lynda's eyes filled with tears she wouldn't yet let fall. There would be time for that later. Now there was still much to be done. She looked to the top of the cliff. If he had gone down anywhere else the crash could have been much worse. Just then she saw the ambulance arrive up top. She told Michael.

He yelled up. "Possible neck and back!"

The paramedics came down the hill carrying a backboard and a neck collar. They carefully immobilized Sean's neck, and then put him onto the backboard. They were about to start the climb up to the ambulance when Sean opened his eyes.

"Mom?"

"I'm right here."

"Is Karen okay?"

"Yes, she's right here too."

He tried to look around. When he realized where he was he looked at his mom and chastised, "What are you doing down here? You have to take care of that baby!"

Lynda stroked the hair on his forehead. "I am taking care of my baby. Don't you worry, we're okay."

"I hurt!"

"Where?" Michael asked. He had been examining Sean closely. He couldn't see any major external injuries, but he couldn't be sure yet.

"My chest, my face. Mom, you were right—airbags do hurt like hell." He closed his eyes. "I kept my hands low and out of the way but my face still hurts."

One of the paramedics said, "You do have some burns on your face from the airbag but they are not too bad."

"Oh."

Karen was only now starting to come out of shock. "Sean, how come you didn't get out? How'd you get your seatbelt on?"

"Hey babe, you okay?"

"I didn't go over a cliff!"

He tried to laugh but coughed instead. "Oh, my chest hurts! I don't know how it all worked. It was like I was in slow motion. My door was jammed again and the edge of the cliff was coming. I asked Dad for help and found myself reaching for the seatbelt with my left hand. With my right, I pulled the parking brake to slow down a bit. Once I got my seatbelt on I tried to hold the door closed. It was like I could hear Dad telling me what to do. Reminding me of everything Mom ever taught me about crashing. Thanks, Pa." He closed his eyes. Lynda's tears began to fall.

The paramedics and the officers carried him up to the ambulance where Michael did a more thorough examination. Lynda and Karen stood side by side watching and clinging to each other's arms. Unbelievably, Sean appeared to have no major injuries. But it was off to the hospital with him to be sure and to take care of the superficial cuts and burns.

"The angels were with him," one officer said to the other.

"And his dad," said Lynda, as she climbed in to go with him to the hospital.

Karen just stood to the side.

"Can she come with us too?" Lynda asked.

"No room."

Michael stepped in and said, "Don't worry Lynda. Karen and I will be right behind you."

Chapter 19

At the hospital Sean had been checked over and was waiting to be released. He was banged up, had minor burns on his face and arms and was bruised and stiff, but okay. Lynda was starting to lose it now that he was safe. She was shaking and the tears started to fall.

"Mom," Sean said, "I'm okay." He was the only patient in a room with two beds separated by curtains. The noise from the action of the hospital intruded slightly into their world.

"I know," she sniffed. She wanted to hold him and not let go. "I'm going to keep a close eye on you for the next few days, to make sure you don't have a concussion."

"Twenty-four hours, Mom, that's what the doc said. That's only one day, not a few days."

"Am I not entitled to a little bit of overprotectiveness?"

"I guess. I mean, you're probably hormonal and all!"

Lynda grabbed a pillow from his bed and hit him with it.

"Nice shot, Mrs. B.," Karen said. Her voice was wobbly and worried.

When Lynda turned to her, she saw Karen's eyes dart to Michael and back to her. Michael's face was unreadable, almost cold. Lynda turned back to her son. She sighed. "I'll be back in a few minutes. I need to talk to Michael. Besides, I am sure you and Karen want some privacy."

As Lynda led Michael out of the room, they heard Sean chuckle softly and say, "Well, we made it, so are you going to jump me now?" and Karen chuckled in response.

"We'll see."

Standing in the bustling hospital hallway with people coming and going, Lynda took a deep breath and forced herself to begin. "This isn't exactly how I imagined telling you this, but there is something important I have to share with you." She forced herself to look into Michael's eyes. Dear God this is hard, she thought. "I'm pregnant," she blurted. She dropped her eyes. Stepping to one side to let people pass she continued, "I wasn't sure when to tell you. I was still worried about the protestors but after talking to Carol and Ron I thought maybe I was making excuses." She was speaking faster and faster. Her hands were talking as much as she was. "I mean, I'm old, I'm high risk, so then I thought I'd wait until I got the results of the CVS because we weren't seeing each other anyway until Sean went off to school, so what was the harm? Then today ..." She paused. She was rambling. She sighed. "I'm sorry. You had a right to know as soon as I did, but I was scared."

Michael stood there looking at her, silent.

"I'm sorry," she said again.

"What are you going to do?" he finally said. He hadn't moved a muscle.

"What do you mean?"

"What do you mean what do I mean? Are you going to have the baby, start over?"

Lynda cocked her head sideways and looked at him as if he were an alien. "Of course I'm having our baby! Don't you want me to?"

Michael exhaled audibly. He still didn't move though. Lynda kept staring at him.

"That's it? That's all you have to say?" Lynda demanded.

"Damn it, woman, I have a ton of questions, but I don't even know if I'm going to get to be a part of my baby's life. If I have to choose between my child and my job!"

"Michael! Don't be a horse's ass! Honestly, what do you take me for?"

"A protective mother!"

"I'm not going to protect our child from her father! Good Lord!" More gently, she added, "And I won't ever ask you to quit your job. I might have some issues to work out but I'll work them out."

Michael closed the distance between them. She was still a little huffy and beautiful. "We'll work them out together."

Lynda snuggled into his embrace. She started to cry and then her whole body shook with sobs as she let out all of her worry from the day.

"Shh, babe, it's going to be okay. We'll be okay. Sean'll be okay. You'll see." He stroked her hair.

"I worried so much about the calls and the clinic but the real danger came anyway and from out of nowhere." As her tears began to subside she lightly punched his chest. "And you didn't even ask me to marry you."

"Without a ring and appropriate wooing, Sean would kick my ass."

"Good answer," Lynda said.

"The truth is, I wasn't sure you'd say yes."

"Men!" she said, exasperated.

Lynda blew her nose and cleaned up her face before she and Michael went back to Sean's room, where they found Sean and Karen lying beside each other, kissing on the bed.

Lynda cleared her throat. Karen jumped to get off the bed but Sean held her beside him as Lynda motioned her to stay put.

"It's okay," she said.

"Well?" Sean asked, looking at his mom and Michael, who had his arm protectively around her, which was a good sign.

"Haven't we had enough excitement for one day?" Lynda said teasingly.

"Apparently not, Mom."

She sighed. Michael smiled. "It's kind of funny. When you think about it, really, me getting your mom knocked up. I, of all people, should've known how to be careful."

Lynda groaned. "At least we are in a position to be able to cope with the product of Mr. Super-Sperm over here." She jerked her thumb at Michael.

Karen and Sean looked at each other. "I think they're slap-happy," Karen said.

"Looks that way." He turned to his mom. "So when's the wedding?"

"Umm, Michael hasn't exactly …"

Sean turned his gaze to Michael and arched an eyebrow menacingly while saying, "Really."

"When I propose to your mom, Sean, I'll have a ring and make it romantic and make it about her and me spending the rest of our lives together, not about the baby. There is a right and a wrong way to do these things, you know."

"Good answer, for now," Sean said.

"But no pressure," Karen added sarcastically.

Everyone burst out laughing.

"Well, this isn't exactly what I was expecting," Detective Hughes said from the doorway.

Four happy faces turned to him. The air in the room seemed to drop several degrees. Lynda was the first to find her voice.

"Detective Hughes, I didn't realize you were working on this case. We didn't see you out there."

"I have good news for you. We were able to set up a roadblock and apprehend the driver of a black SUV that was covered in the paint from Sean's car. The suspect is in custody and is writing up their statement as we speak."

"Wow, that's great," Michael said. "That was fast."

"Karen's the reason for that; she gave the officers on the scene good information."

Karen looked stunned. She didn't know what to say. The idea that she had thought quickly and really made a difference made her feel mature and see that she was able to cope in the world in an adult way. She really was going to be okay, in life, she was really going to make it. She'd waited years to feel this way. And now, because of Sean and her love for him, it was here. It was a part of her all along and now she could really see it.

Lynda walked over to Karen and gave her a big hug. "Thank you sweetheart, thank you so much." She took a step back but kept her hands on Karen's shoulders, with tears in her eyes she said, "Not having to worry about the man who did this still being out there is … it's just so huge Karen. I can't express how grateful I am to you."

Sean beamed. "That's my Karen."

"Well done," Michael said. He was sincere and yet strangely taut.

"Yes well done, indeed young lady. People twice your age often don't show as much presence of mind."

Karen glowed.

Detective Hughes continued, "We'll need to take both your and Sean's …" he nodded at the teenagers, "… statements though. I'd like to do that now, if you don't mind. I'll start with you, Sean, if that's all right. Why don't the rest of you wait in the waiting room and I'll be out in a few minutes."

Sean shrugged. "Sure."

In the hallway outside Sean's room Lynda hugged Karen yet again. She had that mother-who-can't-stop-touching-a-child-thing after a near disaster going on. Michael, too, kept a hand on Karen's shoulder and his other on Lynda's back. He needed the contact more than they did. Karen called Maddie and told her about the accident and not to wait for them for the movie.

Ten minutes later, after Detective Hughes had taken Karen aside to get her statement, Michael and Lynda were sitting in chairs in the waiting room when he said to her, "I think he's not telling us everything."

Lynda yawned, exhausted. "Who? Detective Hughes?"

"Yeah."

"He's a cop, Michael. He probably doesn't think we're on a need-to-know basis of whatever it is. Maybe this guy has done this before or something."

Michael had a bad feeling, but he didn't say any more. He just held the sleepy woman who would soon be his wife and stroked her hair. She yawned again.

"Michael …"

"Hmm?"

"Can you come over tonight? I am so tired and I have to check on Sean every two hours tonight for his head injury; I could use the help."

"Sure. I'd better get used to sleepless nights anyway."

She chuckled softly.

"Lynda …"

"Mmm …"

"I don't ever want to be apart from you again."

She sighed contentedly. "That sounds good," she said, barely awake.

"So can I move in with you and Sean?"

He thought she nodded slightly before she fell asleep but he wasn't sure.

A few minutes later, Detective Hughes appeared and asked them to join him with Sean and Karen in Sean's room.

Lynda yawned as she stood up. "Well, whatever it was he wasn't saying, looks like he's about to say it now."

Michael was quiet. He hadn't liked the way Detective Hughes had looked at him. Lynda could feel the tension in his body.

"Babe," she said, "Sean and Karen are okay. They have the guy in custody. It's going to be fine."

He squeezed her close to him, but said nothing. Once they were in Sean's room gathered around his bed, he turned to face Detective Hughes and said, "Okay, we're all here. What is it you have to say?" His voice betrayed his tension.

Detective Hughes nodded. "Perhaps you'll want to sit down for this," he said, looking at Lynda.

Lynda looked at him strangely. She was fully awake now. "Just spit it out. Please."

Karen and Sean were quiet, apprehensive.

Detective Hughes gave a terse nod to Lynda and began. "This wasn't a random act of road rage, I'm afraid." He paused.

Lynda promptly pulled up a chair and sat in it. With effort she managed to force the ringing from ears and focus on Detective Hughes.

Michael said, "This is connected to the clinic?"

"Yes and no."

"That's helpful," he retorted, frustrated. Lynda put her hand on his arm signaling him gently to take a deep breath.

Sean spoke up now. "You mean someone tried to kill Karen and me specifically, on purpose?"

"You, yes. Karen was just in the wrong place at the wrong time."

"Oh my God!" was all Sean could say.

"It was a woman!" Karen said. "The laughter, I remember now. It was a woman's voice."

Sean, Lynda, and Michael turned to look at her, then to Detective Hughes for confirmation.

He nodded. "Yes. It was someone you know Dr. Cameron. Someone you know quite well."

Michael stared at the detective.

"Someone you know, too, Mrs. Blake."

Lynda just looked at him, "But who would want to hurt Sean?"

The detective continued, "Sean was really just a means to an end." He looked at Michael waiting for the light to dawn. "It was Susan Costas."

"From the clinic?" Sean said.

Michael nodded mutely. He felt his whole world rock beneath him. Should he have known? Should he have seen this coming? Was this his fault for leading her on before then rejecting her? Had he led her on? Probably. He hadn't meant to but he'd been so lonely and she was there. God, he'd been so selfish, so wrapped up in himself, his loss he hadn't even thought about Susan until he'd already hurt her. When would he learn that caring about someone, even Susan, meant actually thinking about things from their perspective? He'd been a lousy friend to her and now Sean was in the hospital.

"And the calls, the graffiti, all of it?" Michael asked.

"The last round of vandalism was not her, maybe not the first either, but she has confessed to the calls to you up at the vineyard and to Lynda."

"That bitch tried to kill my son!"

Michael's world was spiraling out of control.

"Mom, I'm okay!" Sean said, alarmed at the venom in his mother's voice. "Calm down, okay? Think of the baby."

She turned to him and then to Detective Hughes. "What about filing a false a police report or whatever it's called? When she claimed she had harassing phone calls?"

"She'll be charged with that too, don't worry, Lynda. We've got her."

"But why would she go to such extremes? It's just all so crazy," Michael said. He was desperate to understand. This was a woman he had loved, lived with; a woman he'd worked with every day for years.

"Love," said Karen.

"Money," said Detective Hughes.

"Money?" they all said, surprised.

"Apparently the guy she left you for, Doc, was a class-A con man. He took her for everything she had. She has a ton of credit-card debt and is barely able to make ends meet. She was facing bankruptcy and she flipped out."

Michael nodded. "She would. She grew up poor, really, really poor, and the thought of going back to that would send her into a panic." He paused. They were all watching him. His voice was so quiet and sad. "When she was a kid her mom lived on nothing, spent what they had on booze, was always looking for a new man to make things better. Sometimes she barely ate at all. That's why she's so ambitious, why she always wanted me to expand the practice."

"That's why she wanted you back," Detective Hughes said. "Financial stability."

"But why go after Sean? Why not come after me?" Lynda asked.

"She's one sick puppy, Mrs. B. I bet she wanted you to suffer for having dared to take Michael from her," Karen said.

Detective Hughes nodded, acknowledging the possibility.

Lynda put her head in her hands. Michael was rigid. He said to Detective Hughes, "What can we expect now? What comes next?"

Detective Hughes filled them in on the timeline of the legal processes. Susan would probably enter a guilty plea, and then go straight to sentencing. He said he'd keep in touch. There was really nothing for them to do at this point. Susan would remain in custody. She wouldn't be able to hurt them again.

Michael nodded, then turned to Sean. "Sean," he said, "I am so sorry. And Karen," he said looking directly at her, "I am so very sorry. I'm just relieved that you both are okay."

Lynda watched him carefully while he was speaking. She stood up and held him. He hugged her back perfunctorily, not nearly as tightly as she would have liked.

Sean looked at Michael. "What are you apologizing for?"

"Yeah," Karen said, "you didn't do anything."

He exhaled and looked down. "But, if it weren't for me, none of this would have happened."

The teenagers turned to Lynda. She smiled at them. She took Michael by the shoulders and made him look at her. "Now that's enough of that!"

"But ..."

"Enough!" she ordered. "This is not your doing or your fault, so don't take on the guilt."

Then with tears in his eyes, he hugged her and held her so tightly she was afraid he'd break one of her ribs. It was going to be the two of them against the world from now on. He could feel it.

"So," Lynda said when he finally let go. "Any more jealous ex-wives or girlfriends I should know about?"

"No, thank God!"

They both laughed.

"So I guess you won't be naming the baby Susan, huh?" Sean said. Everyone laughed out loud.

"I guess not!" Lynda said. She turned to Detective Hughes. "Thanks for everything." She walked over to him and hugged him. He tried not to look embarrassed.

"I'm just glad everything turned out all right," he said.

"Us too."

"Congratulations, by the way. I wondered when you came to see me last time if you were pregnant. I thought so, but it didn't seem right to ask. I am happy for you, Mrs. Blake."

"Hey, what about me?" piped in Michael.

"Doc, you are one lucky sonofabitch. Treat her right, you hear me?"

Michael grinned from ear to ear. "Yes sir!"

"Good. Take care. I'll be in touch." And with that he left the four of them to each other.

"Let's go home," Sean said.

Michael left to find the doctor who could sign him out. He ran into Paul and Maddie at the nurses' station. He reassured them that everyone was okay and pointed them in the right direction. A moment later he heard Paul's sarcastic, "Well I guess this is a good reason for standing us up. But Dude, I want details." Tired laughter and groans followed. Karen and Sean began the first of many retellings of their ordeal.

Chapter 20

Days passed, weeks passed, and life settled into a new routine. Detective Hughes called to say that Susan had in fact entered a plea of guilty and would remain in custody while awaiting sentencing. Sean recovered with no complications. Michael moved in. Karen seemed to have too, though Lynda tried to make sure she slept in the guest room. She and Michael kept a close eye on her. Something was wrong at home, Lynda was sure of that. She was not the school slut anymore, but the reasons she had taken that route in the first place were still unclear, at least to Lynda.

Lynda continued to expand. Gradually the nausea eased off and more food cravings crept in. She still didn't have an engagement ring. Michael was attentive and kind and content after having moved in. Work was crazy for him with Susan being gone. He had a temp helping out until he could hire someone else. She was sure that was the only thing causing the delay. At least she hoped she was sure. Maybe day-to-day life was too unromantic especially, with her ever-increasing girth, but he was here at least. That had to be enough for now.

One night when Karen was again up late watching Letterman, Michael came downstairs to concoct a mixture of chocolate ice cream, Karo syrup and maraschino cherries for his pregnant woman upstairs. He plopped down of the sofa adjacent to Karen. She smiled at him. She yawned. "So," she said getting right to the point, " When are you going to pop the question? We're all waiting."

"Well," he hesitated. "I will tell you this much—if you can keep a secret, that is."

Karen laughed out loud despite herself, "Umm, yeah Michael I think we all know that I can keep a secret. What? Tell me!"

"I'm picking up the ring tomorrow after work. It's finally ready."

"Is it custom made?"

"Yeah, I designed it myself. I hope to God she likes it."

"Nice, Michael, very classy. I'm sure she'll love it." Karen yawned again and stretched. "I'll make sure Sean and I are scarce tomorrow night."

He smiled. "Thanks. I'm going to tell Sean in the morning, kind of ask for her hand, you know? Then I'll make her a romantic dinner full of every sort of food to meet her cravings, speaking of which, I better get the ice cream she sent me for and bring it up to her."

As he stood up and was about to head to the kitchen, Karen stood up too and gave him a quick hug.

"Thanks, Michael, for everything." They both knew what she meant.

"Sure," he said. "Anytime." He paused. "Does Lynda know yet?" he asked. He knew the answer of course but he hoped to prompt Karen into telling so he no longer had to keep this secret from her.

"You mean you haven't told her?" Karen was shocked.

"Of course I haven't told her Karen. Not without you telling me I could. I mean I want to of course. She's more than a little curious about why Sean won't let you go home. Lord knows he's tried to finesse it so she won't see that's how he really feels but she's not stupid. But this is Lynda we're talking about she might actually die of curiosity but she will respect both his and your privacy and trust that one of you will come to her when you're ready."

Karen laughed. She was usually so observant about people but somehow she had totally missed this. "Go ahead Michael, tell her with my blessing. I'll talk to her tomorrow myself." She exhaled. This was actually getting a little easier with time. "You know, I've been kind of wondering, I mean I know things are a little nuts for you at work and well I guess I was wondering if I could maybe work at the clinic a couple of afternoons a week. I can do filing and stuff. I'd like to learn more about the business to see if this something I might like to do after college. What do you think?"

"I think that'd be awesome. I would love to show you the business. Your working at the clinic would really be helping me out in fact." He grinned, yes he thought to himself this could work out well for both of them. "What would you think about doing some peer counseling too?"

"Gee I don't know. Maybe. Can I think about it?"

"Sure. Take all the time you need. How about working Tuesdays and Thursdays from four to six? You'll be a Godsend helping me catch up."

Karen smiled and said, "Sounds great. I can't wait. Thanks Michael." They said goodnight and Karen turned off the TV and headed to her room for the night.

Maybe he was going to be okay at this parenting thing after all. At least he wasn't going to have to do it alone; he'd always have Lynda right there with him.

When he went upstairs to deliver the craving du jour, Lynda was sitting up in bed looking concerned.

"So, how is she?"

"She's okay. What did you hear?"

Lynda held her hands out for the ice cream. She dug into it as if she were starving. "Nothing really. I just hoped she was finally opening up to one of us. Clearly Sean knows something. I figure her dad abused her, and she just isn't ready to share it with me yet."

Michael nodded. "She talked to me when we were up at the vineyard actually, I was in the right place at the right time you know, and I've helped her find someone to talk to. I've been dying to tell you but I just couldn't. She actually figured I already had, can you believe that."

"He did more than hit her?"

He nodded.

"Bastard!"

He nodded, amazed at how she could eat and talk at the same time so neatly.

"Sean knows. He found out the night of the accident, right?"

Michael said, "Yes, I think that's when she told him."

Lynda nodded. "Makes sense. I guess he must have handled it pretty well. No wonder he's not letting her go back there. I'm okay with that, are you?"

"Of course."

"Good." Lynda exhaled. "Well, my family sure has changed this year."

"For the better, I hope," Michael said.

"Oh yes," she said, "I have excellent taste in strays!"

Michael took the empty bowl from Lynda and put it on the bedside table. "So you really liked that disgusting concoction?" He straddled the lovely lady in bed.

"Mmm, it was delicious. You should've had some."

"Well, I couldn't very well take it out of your beautiful mouth now, could I?" He kissed her eyelids, her nose, her lips. "Mmm, you're sticky." He deepened his kiss. "Hey, this doesn't taste bad!"

Lynda laughed. "See, I told you so!"

Michael proceeded to cherish every inch of her ever-expanding flesh as he made love to the woman he wanted to grow old with, the one he wanted to grow with. As they lay spent in each other's arms afterward, he said to her, "Think you'll still want to make love to me when we're eighty?"

"Definitely, and you'd better still want me, mister."

He nuzzled behind her ear. "No doubt about that!"

Lynda smiled, yawned, and said, "Good."

The next day was a busy one for Michael. After having Sean's "It's about damn time" ringing in his ears, he was off to work.

Carol had chosen a few hard-to-screw-up recipes for him. Grocery shopping filled his lunch hour. After work he raced to the jeweler's to pick up the ring, then hurried back to the house to start cooking dinner. The recipes were from his new favorite cookbook: 365 20-minute Recipes. Quick Coq au Vin being the main dish, with salad and Betty Crocker butter and herb mashed potatoes, with vanilla ice cream and cherries jubilee for dessert.

When Lynda came home from her day of working on her manuscript at the library, the house was alive with the smell of frying bacon and onions and the sound of birch logs crackling in the fireplace. Only the fire lighted the library, and the light danced over the blanket and pillows Michael had set up for an indoor picnic. A single red rose lay on top of a note on one of the pillows.

Lynda picked up the rose and inhaled its scent deeply before she picked up the note. It read:

> My dearest Lynda,
>
> You are invited to a romantic firelight picnic at 7:30
>
> p.m. this evening.
>
> M

Lynda smiled and went upstairs to wash her face and get ready for dinner. At exactly 7:30 she was waiting for Michael dressed in an elegant floor-length negligee. It was royal blue with lace on the bodice being stretched by her more-ample-than-usual bosom. She had powdered herself in honey dust and shimmered in the firelight.

Michael almost dropped the salads he was carrying when he saw her there waiting for him. He was wearing a dark gray sweater with the sleeves pushed up on his forearms, which accentuated his strong arms and shoulders, and black jeans that hugged his thighs.

"Wow, Lynda," he said as he joined her on the floor, "you look so beautiful tonight." His voice was deep and husky.

Despite herself she blushed. "You look pretty amazing yourself. To what do I owe the honor of this evening?" She had her hopes high but was happy to wait, happy to let Michael run the show tonight.

He smiled. "This is because I love you."

"I could get used to this, you know."

"I intend to see to exactly that."

All through dinner Michael itched to touch her, to taste her, but he waited. And she seemed content to wait. They talked about the baby coming and Sean going and work and life.

After Michael cleared away the last of the dishes he returned with a blue velvet box. He got down on his knees before Lynda. He took her hands in his. As he opened the box he said, "Lynda, my love, I want to live all of my life loving you as your husband. I want to wake up next to you every day and fall asleep holding you every night. I want to raise our child with you and retire with you. I want my whole world to begin and end with you. Will you please do me the honor of becoming my wife?"

With tears running down her cheeks Lynda kissed him. "Yes," she said, "oh yes!"

Michael took the three-stone diamond ring, set in dual bands of platinum and gold out of the box and placed it on her left hand.

"Oh, Michael, it's so beautiful." She held out her hand as she studied the ring. "I've never seen anything like it!"

He smiled. "I designed it with the help of an old college friend who is a jeweler. The gold and the platinum of the band represent us. We are two strong individuals who are stronger together but we won't lose who we are. The three diamonds are for the past we will create, the moment we live and the future we will always have."

Lynda caressed his cheeks as she kissed him again. "I love it! I love you!"

"I was going crazy waiting for it to be ready. So many times I've wanted to beg you to marry me!"

She laughed at that. "I was wondering what was taking so long, but I forced myself to be patient and I'm glad I did. This was the perfect proposal. Thank you! I can't wait to tell our daughter …"

"Or son …"

"… how romantic her daddy was when he asked me to marry him."

"Now that we are at long last betrothed, can we please have a short engagement and get right to the marriage part? " he begged.

"Sure, but I need at least a couple of weeks to find the perfect dress. We can call Reverend Mitchell in the morning and set a date."

*   *   *   *   *

Four harried weeks later they were married at the vineyard. They honeymooned in Half Moon Bay. It boasted a luxury hotel and spa but was still close to home, just in case something happened and Sean or Karen needed them.

And several months later, arriving healthy and right on time, was a beautiful baby girl. MJ, Mary Joan Cameron, weighed in at eight pounds, two ounces, with a shock of dark hair and, of course, beautiful blue eyes. Mother and daughter were doing well. The father survived the experience but gave the nurses much to gossip and chuckle about because of his nerves. Sean and Karen arrived at the hospital just before little MJ was born and were the first to visit. Sean was almost afraid to hold her, but once he did he almost didn't give her back.

Lynda looked at her son adoring his sister; looked around the room at her loving husband and Karen, her other daughter, and she started to cry.

"Look at this."

They all turned to her.

"Look at us. Look at my family. God has blessed me so much with all of you. I never thought … I mean, after David died, I never thought I'd know this kind of joy again."

Michael kissed her on her tear-stained cheek. Karen hugged her and Sean reluctantly gave MJ back, then kissed his mom on the cheek.

"It's like you always told me, Mom. Life is for living and living is for loving. It just took you a while to follow your own advice, that's all."

K.L. McLoughlin

About the Author

K. L. Mc Loughlin did her undergraduate work at
Carleton University in Ottawa, Ontario (Canada) and received her
Master's in Education from Lesley University
in Cambridge, Massachusetts (USA).

After living in the San Francisco Bay Area
for eight years, she now lives in
Victoria, British Columbia (Canada) where she is
working on her second book.

For more information visit:
www.klmcloughlin.com